FAREWELL MY HEART

A NOVEL BY

FERENC MOLNAR

Translated by Elinor Rice

SIMON AND SCHUSTER 1945

ABOUT THE APPEARANCE OF BOOKS
IN WARTIME

A ruling by the War Production Board has curtailed the use of paper by book publishers.

In line with this ruling and in order to conserve materials and manpower, we are co-operating by:

1. Using lighter-weight paper, which reduces the bulk of our books substantially.

2. Printing books with smaller margins and with more words to each page. Result fewer pages per book.

Slimmer and smaller books save paper and plate metal and labor. We are sure that readers will understand the publishers' desire to co-operate as fully as possible with the objectives of the War Production Board and our government.

MANUFACTURED IN THE UNITED STATES OF AMERICA
BY H. WOLFF BOOK MFG. CO., N. Y.

CHAPTER ONE

R ELIGION?" THE Italian officer in the Fascist uniform
asked, holding my passport in his hand.

The train had been standing at the border station
between Switzerland and Italy for a long time. The
name of the station was painted on a board: Domodossola. Outside, the winter afternoon was growing dim.
Such silence reigned over the station that you could
hear the steps of another soldier in Fascist uniform,
nerve-rackingly clear, as he paced back and forth on
the deserted platform.

"Religion?"

My face grew warm. I must have been blushing,
because suddenly I could sense the warmth rising up
to my cheekbones. The Hungarian consul general in
Paris had smiled at me meaningfully as he made out
my passport. Without my asking him to, he had left
blank the heading marked "Religion," which by then
had become so important a classification on all Hungarian passports. That was why the Fascist officer was
surveying me now, questioning and suspicious.

"Jew," I answered.

"Why isn't it on your passport?"

"Because they didn't write it in," I said.

"Why not?"

1

"Out of consideration," I said. "I was a journalist of some standing in my own country. The consul wanted to do me a favor."

The officer shrugged his shoulders. "Where's the favor in that?"

He went on turning the pages of my passport. He came to the American visa.

"You're going to America?"

"Yes."

"Where from?"

"Genoa."

"When?"

"Tomorrow noon."

He flipped my passport closed, and put it down with the pile he'd collected from the other passengers on the train.

"You'll get it back before you reach Milan," he said roughly.

I had the feeling that he would have liked to go to America too, but realized it was impossible, and was angry at the whole idea and at me because I could go there and he couldn't. The American visitor's visa had been in my passport for eleven months. Since then I had traveled over many European borders. And at every border the poor, underpaid passport officials had stared with that same strange expression at the American visa. As if it were some foreign coin which, though it had no value in their own country, they felt was very valuable. The officer went on into the next car with the pile of passports. Three soldiers followed him.

All four wore huge revolvers over their stomachs. The train began to move again in the direction of Milan and Genoa. It was almost dark by then. In our compartment, two electric bulbs lit up sadly, weakly.

After this short scene, which revealed so much about me to my traveling companions, I looked around. I had two companions. When I got on at Geneva, I had been alone in the compartment. My first fellow traveler, a pretty, young girl with red hair, got on at Lausanne. The second, an elderly, well-dressed man, at Montreux. The Italian officer had examined their passports before mine. In the short interchange which usually accompanies a passport inspection, I had discovered that the elderly gentleman was a Finnish consul and that the red-haired girl was a countrywoman of mine, a Hungarian. Up to now I had not spoken a word to them. The consul had begun to talk to the girl as soon as he got on at Montreux, after she had answered his greeting with an encouraging smile. Since then they had exchanged a word now and then. But I had sat in my corner since early morning, absorbed in a book, and when I was not reading I pretended I was, and when I grew tired of that, I closed my eyes and pretended I was asleep. I don't like making acquaintances on trains. Now, unexpectedly, the consul addressed me in French.

"Stupid, this sniffing into religion," he said with a scornful smile.

"Yes," I answered.

"A shame and a disgrace," he added without any

sign of indignation. "In the twentieth century! 1939! Yes, and what's more . . ."

He glanced at his watch.

"In seven hours we'll be saying 1940."

For no reason, the red-haired girl laughed. "Tomorrow is New Year's!"

"A sad new year," the consul said. "A sad new year for us Finns."

We were silent. The girl looked at me. For a moment our eyes met. I sighed. I thought I was sighing from boredom, as one sometimes does alone on a long train trip, after an extended silence. Now I know that was not the reason I sighed. There are certain women who, when they look at you for the first time, have something familiar in their eyes. As if you had known them for ten or fifteen years. Or there is something in their eyes, some reason why from now on you are going to know them for ten or fifteen years. I felt something like that when our eyes met. Not right away—but an hour or so later I felt it with complete clarity. Even though I was fifty-two and had already gathered from the girl's conversation that she was only twenty-one. She began to talk to the consul again, while he—I don't know any better way to put it—devoured her with his eyes. This interested me because, when I looked more carefully at the girl, I noticed that there was nothing unusual enough about her to explain the consul's ardent, almost loving gaze. Certainly, I decided, there was something unusual about the consul. There are some aging men whom the mere breath of a

very young girl throws into ecstasy. Nothing so unusual about that. I looked out of the window. They
went on talking to each other.

A dancer. Emigrating. Comes of a good family.
Father was a lawyer in the provinces. She was one of
six children. Father committed suicide. He had red
hair, too, almost the same shade as hers. She inherited
her nose from her father, too. A pretty, turned-up little
nose. Her mouth was not small—I like that. The most
remarkable thing about her was her eyes. I never
saw such a quick, lively look. Her eyes lit rapidly, spar-
klingly, on one spot after another. When, from time
to time during the conversation, she looked at me, the
stranger, it happened so quickly that afterwards I could
not be sure she had looked at me at all.

Once after a long pause, she said to the consul, "I'm
not a Jew."

"I didn't ask if you were," the consul answered,
laughing.

"Oh, well," she said, "I only mentioned it because
sometimes when people first see me they think I am."

No, she's not a Jew. But she's left Hungary because
everything that meant anything to her in Budapest has
crumbled to the ground. The relatives who brought
her up have gone to South America. The Jewish movie
people, the night-club and café owners disappeared
one after another from Budapest. Afterward letters
came from them from Paris, from America. She had
three managers herself, who used to give her engage-
ments at their places, who went to Cuba, Montevideo,

and Rio de Janeiro. The audiences have changed, too. God knows what the future will bring. She isn't a Jew, but please don't think for a moment she's pointing it out because she's anti-Semitic. She isn't. Oh, not in the least.

She was looking at me now. I realized that this unasked and unwelcome kindliness had made me blush.

She is going to America. She wants a career.

"And, of course, you'll have one," the consul said.

She has a relative in Chicago, a cousin of her mother's, who sent her an affidavit. At the Hungarian border, the police took down her hair to see whether she was smuggling out any jewels in its thick shrubbery. She had none. She didn't need any. But she would have them.

"Oh, of course," the consul said.

"How do you know?"

"I can sense it. I only have to look at a young girl once to know what's going to become of her."

"What will become of me?" The girl smiled at him, showing healthy, strong teeth.

"You'll have a career," the consul announced with a stupid-serious expression.

Yes, she wants a career, and she'll have one. She knows it, she feels it. Most of all she wants to dance. In New York and in Hollywood. Preferably Hollywood, though. In the movies or not, but in Hollywood. Inadvertently I glanced at her legs, which her short skirt so generously revealed. She looked, lightning-quick, into my eyes again. With difficulty I stifled a second sigh. After fifty, a man may sigh, too, because the girl who looks at him seems too young compared to him. The Finnish consul was giving her advice, during which he put his hand on her thigh over her lovely round knee. I wished she would push away his old hand with its bulging veins. But she didn't push it away. Perhaps she didn't even notice the gesture. (A pity that today I can still set down the sentence: "Perhaps she didn't even notice the gesture." And if she had noticed it!)

The train stopped. Stresa. You could see the lake sparkling in the darkness. A few pitiful lights glowed on the islands. I was here ten years ago. The lake was blue then; a thousand windows gleamed in the world-famous hotels; the evening air tasted of fruits and flowers; in the electric radiance of the station, rich, well-dressed men chatted in many languages and laughed with lovely ladies. Now only three gaping, shabby Italian soldiers stood stupidly on the platform, motionless under a lamp. The windows were dark. A railroad hand shoved a wheelbarrow around the station building, and disappeared. The Finnish consul was silent, and gazed with staring eyes darkly ahead of him. He seemed to be remembering again that at this moment his fatherland was in the midst of its bitterest struggle with the Russians. The train did not move. The three soldiers stood as motionless, goggling at the train with as little expression, as if they were wax figures or dead men stood up on their feet. It might have been the promise of the American visa in my passport and the ship's passage in my pocket, but I had the feeling that all Europe was dead, my former life was dead, the Finnish consul was dead, the three soldiers standing on the platform were dead, too—nobody was alive but this red-haired girl who was now definitely, and with insistent impudence, staring into my eyes again.

CHAPTER TWO

IN THE evening there was a two-hour wait at Milan for the train to Genoa. My program included dinner in the station restaurant at Milan. I know of no bigger restaurant in any station in Europe. A medium-sized cathedral could be stored inside it. On this evening, December 31, 1939, the restaurant was practically empty. I don't know why, even now. It is one of the most popular restaurants in Milan, and December 31 is no worse a day for restaurants in Europe than it is in America. At three or four tables, people were dining. I took one of the empty tables, the Finnish consul and the red-haired girl another. They came into the restaurant after I did, and when they passed my table, they didn't greet me, merely looked at me. The girl smiled a little, almost warmly, as though she were thinking, "Why don't we all three have dinner at the same table?" The consul threw me a cold glance, perhaps because the girl's smile was warm. I distinctly felt that the consul considered me his rival, although he must have realized that I didn't know the red head at all. They sat down fairly far away from me, and later I saw that they were drinking a large bottle of Italian red wine with their dinner. They laughed and talked loudly, but in that enormous place there was

9

such an echo that I couldn't understand a word they said. I was certain they would stay together. Only I didn't know whether it would be here in Milan—or whether I would meet them again next day on the *Rex*, the ship going to America.

Four waiters were standing in front of my table. They were staring at my traveling bag, which stood on the floor beside me, and envying me because I was going to America. (I spent several years traveling through Europe from one country to another; and I discovered that in longing for America, Italians hold first place. The Germans, who were—incredible as it seems today—the greatest admirers of America in Europe, only hold second place.) The waiters were bewailing Italy's ruin.

"We're through!" they said. "Up to now the whole world loved us; now nobody loves us: There's no more tourist travel in Italy. Neither the English nor the Americans come any more."

"Only the Germans," a fat little bald head, who looked like a clown, said hoarsely.

They laughed about the Germans, and the clown cleverly imitated the accent with which Germans struggled to order food in Italian.

"You can be glad you haven't been dragged into the war," I said.

One of them shook his fist furiously.

"What good is it," he almost screamed, "when 600,000 men are mobilized and kept in barracks?"

I tried, unsuccessfully, to explain to him that these 600,000 were still alive. I advised him to save his fist-shaking for the time when . . .

"You have it easy," he said reproachfully. "You're going to America. We've got to stay here."

They left me alone at the table. But they stayed together, and I saw them again, far away near the door, when I went back to the train. They were still sticking together, the same four, and still going on with their argument. And one was shaking his fist, just as he had before.

In the Genoa train I found an unheated, unfriendly, empty compartment, and sat down in the corner. I thought about the red-haired girl whom I had left back there in the big, empty restaurant with the consul. I didn't even look toward their table as I went out. Would I ever see her again? I knew, I had overheard, that she was going to America, but I didn't know when she was sailing. Perhaps she would enjoy herself with the consul in Milan for a few days. Or a few weeks. In this short time, the consul had become deeply en-meshed with the girl, that seemed clear. And she liked being with the consul, too; it wasn't hard to see that. Perhaps she wouldn't go to America at all. Was it pos-sible that such an accidental meeting with a stranger in a railway compartment could change her whole life's plan? Are there such accidents? And, if there are, why in hell should I concern myself with her affairs?

When I had reached this point in my thoughts, she

strolled down the train corridor, past the glass in my compartment door. Not with the consul. Alone. She looked through the glass, stopped there for a second, then, with no change of expression, went on. I knew she would stroll back and come into my compartment. I knew it without question. Somehow—just because she appeared at the moment I was thinking about her —I considered this unknown girl mine, my property, who forever after would come where I willed her to. I thought of the airplanes which, I had read, could be directed from a distance by radio beams. It was an entirely unfounded, childish feeling, but strange—I might almost say, exalted.

After a minute I discovered I was right. I saw her walk back along the corridor and stop in front of the glass door again. She opened the door and called in, "May I sit here?"

I was so embarrassed that instead of a spoken answer I indicated with a gesture that she should take a seat beside me. I was disturbed, because it seemed as if my stupid thought, that I was capable of directing the girl by beams, was not pure imagination. I indicated the seat with my hand, since I was afraid my voice might break, or sound hoarse, if I answered.

She brought her two small suitcases in, and sat down beside me. I think this is the second time I have mentioned that then, in 1939, I was fifty-two years old. I was as embarrassed as an eighteen-year-old boy going to bed for the first time with the girl he loves. I've already said, too, that the girl was pretty. I would like to be precise, though; that's why I emphasize now that she was not beautiful. Just that she was about as pretty as hundreds, or perhaps thousands, of others. I have reported truly and faithfully what I had learned about her in the few hours we had traveled together. What I saw, what I heard. Certainly nothing remarkable. Nothing in the least remarkable, nothing interesting. And still, when she sat down beside me and said softly, "It's cold," and pushed closer to me, and her shoulder and hip touched me, I felt unerringly that we two belonged to each other for all that remained of life. This was a fearful new element in my existence, this suddenly born thought which had taken possession of me with such overwhelming force, for no reason at all. Somewhere I read once that the bubonic plague seizes men suddenly like that. I could have wept for rage, despair, and joy. There was a second in that first strange moment when it passed through my mind that perhaps I had gone mad. She was pretty, I've said so already—let's be absolutely frank, she was conventionally pretty—and let's be even franker, there was something in her character, in her appearance, in her look, in her voice, that was reminiscent of the typical Budapest streetwalker. I'm not afraid to set this down about her. I do not feel I am insulting her by it, because never in my life have I loved anyone, neither woman nor man, more than I loved her. But I want to put all my thoughts honestly on paper; that is my only aim now.

The girl touched my forehead. The skin of her hand

was soft and white. She pushed back the lock of hair that always falls over my right eye, as if she wanted to scrutinize my face more closely.

"Who are you? It's as if I'd seen you in Budapest."

I still didn't dare to speak aloud. I reached in my pocket and handed her my passport. She read it all through carefully. Then gave it back.

"That's an original way of introducing yourself," she remarked. "No deceit. Everything above board."

She looked in turn at the photograph in the passport and at me. As if she wanted to match the original to the picture, like a border guard.

"Fifty-two?" she asked.

"Yes."

"You don't look it."

"Thanks."

I was growing braver.

"Now we'll have a look at your passport," I said.

She handed me her passport. Edith Gaal. Actress, 21 years old.

"Actress?"

"No."

"What then?"

"A dancer. The police were nice enough to write actress on my passport. Sounds more respectable when a person's so young."

I gave her back the passport.

"It's very cold," she said, and squeezed close to me. She gazed up into my eyes, with the look I have since come to know meant, "Kiss me."

Instead, I asked, "Did the consul stay in Milan?"

"Yes."

"And you."

"I'm going to America."

"When?"

"Tomorrow noon. With you."

"What do you mean—with me?"

"On the *Rex*."

"With me and three hundred others."

"No. Only seventy-two altogether."

"How do you know?"

"They told me at the travel bureau at Lausanne. Just an intimate little group."

She came back to the consul.

"The consul is rich. He wanted to take me with him."

"Where?"

"Madrid. South America."

I barked at her like a police captain.

"Don't mix things up. Was it Madrid or South America?"

"Anywhere. He was in love with me."

"And you?"

She looked at me indignantly.

"You don't suppose I was interested in him as a man? He could have been my father."

"How old is he?"

She tore her eyes suddenly from mine and, embarrassed, began to rummage in her pocketbook for her handkerchief. You could tell she had made a slip. And in that instant it wasn't hard to guess that the consul was either exactly my age or a year or two younger. Just to torture myself and her, I repeated the question.

"How old is he?"

But she had already recovered her presence of mind. She snapped her pocketbook closed, and lied calmly.

"Sixty. Or more. I don't know."

"And even so—he fell in love with you so suddenly?"

"Oh," she said—and distorted her full lips bitterly—"people only fall in love with me like that. Suddenly and violently. The ones who know me and are with me a lot don't need me. But with you I'm going to be careful."

I stared at her in astonishment.

"You're going to be what?"

"Careful, so you won't get tired of me."

I still didn't understand.

"*What* are you going to do?"

"I'm going to be very careful with you, so that everything will stay just as it is this minute."

I tried to make my lips produce something that might resemble a mocking smile. I don't know how it came off. I only know that, at that moment, in my dreams America was full of this girl. How much I had thought about America before I went into exile, how much I had read and inquired, how much I had learned about America! How many plans I had! My suitcase was full of notes. How many addresses I had taken down! How many excellent maps I had! And of all that, there now remained only this unknown, warm, red-haired girl. A thought obsessed me which I finally put into words, "Where she is is America." It didn't make much sense, but it did me good to repeat that sentence over and over in my head. Then I said to myself, "She is the future." Again, for an instant, I believed I had gone mad. But never in my life have I loved anyone as I did that girl at that moment. And I never loved her more than at that moment when, in the dark, icy winter evening, the train began to wind through the street lights of Genoa, and gradually slowed down.

We picked up our wraps and stood with our bags in the corridor. In some way, somehow, the girl must have seen through my skull into my brain.

"Do you love me?" she asked softly.

The amazing thing is that at that instant the question seemed neither foolish nor unexpected. It did not surprise me. I didn't answer. The train stopped. We got off.

It was terribly cold. The big hotel they had recommended to me was across from the station, a few minutes away. I started out on foot, carrying my own and one of the girl's suitcases. The steamship company would take care of our larger luggage in the morning. It was a nasty, cold, unfriendly winter evening in Genoa. The hotel lobby wasn't friendly, either. It was only half lighted. We went up to the desk. A clerk shoved a form in front of me, for me to fill out.

The girl grabbed my arm.

"Let's take a double room," she said simply.

The clerk could not understand. She was speaking Hungarian.

"Why?" I asked stupidly.

"Oh, don't worry," she said seriously, "not for *that*. Only for economy."

I filled out the form mechanically, as if in a dream.

"A double room," the girl told the clerk.

She gave the bags to the bellboy, and the key, too.

"Take the things up. We're going to a café for a while."

She hung onto my arm and practically carried me out into the street, down the wide steps of the hotel.

"Don't look so frightened," she said. "This isn't the first time I've spent the night in a room with a man, without letting him touch me. You won't touch me. You won't even come near me. *I* swear it—not you. Your word wouldn't mean much. *I* swear it."

She added simply, "I'm a virgin."

She took a few steps down the street, then immediately stopped.

"I don't want to lose my virginity—not today or in this way."

"And not by me," I said, putting on an air of self-deprecation.

She walked on. Shrugged her shoulders.

"I didn't say that," she said.

CHAPTER THREE

NEVER BEFORE had I lived through such a joyless, frightened New Year's Eve as that one. A frightened city in a frightened land, around which rolled the lightning and thunder of war, and which feared that all too soon it, too, would have to play a part in the great European drama. Hardly a person walked on the wide boulevard. Students in their many-colored caps, arm in arm, set off little firecrackers on the sidewalks. We glanced into a couple of coffeehouses, but turned away quickly. Inside were huddled sad, half-lighted groups, bundled in their winter coats. Finally we asked a policeman, who showed us the way to a big, lively bar. It was crowded and noisy; it was warm and it smelled. So we drank a glass of *grappa*, and went back to the hotel. Now only half of the half-lights were burning in the lobby. But at least it was good and warm.

"Is there a bar in the hotel?" the girl asked.

Instead of answering, the uniformed night porter stood up immediately, and beckoned us to follow him. He led us through zigzagging hallways into an absolutely empty bar, behind whose counter a white-coated bartender was fast asleep, with the evening paper still in his hand.

We had something to eat and some more to drink.

19

The girl drank more than I did. You could tell it by looking at her. She became livelier and prettier. She sat beside me in a booth, and leaned against me. Her hair had a natural scent, very individual and unlike the scent of any other woman's hair. In my nose's experience, dark, blonde, and red heads generally have natural hair odors of three absolutely distinct types, without much individual difference. I have a terrifically sensitive nose. When I was a child and my mother had nine or ten women in for coffee of an afternoon, if I came home from school and sniffed through the nine or ten fur coats in the foyer, I could tell exactly who her guests were. I only mention this now to explain why the scent of the girl's hair always excited me so, up to the very end. I can't describe exactly what the scent was like, even though it is in my nose, or my nose's memory, for as long as I live. It was not a flower scent, and it was nothing that could be compared to the scent of synthetic perfumes. It was not a human body scent, either. I dare admit that if I had noticed it in anyone else I would not have said it was a particularly pleasant smell. It was a worse than indifferent smell. It had something provocative and irritating about it. It affected me somewhat like those poisonous plants which the men of certain savage African tribes chew. And they are driven mad, and dance drunkenly, and—I saw it in a scientific movie once—bite their partners' shoulders and breasts. Whenever she forced that great, thick, red bush, which she wore on her head, under my nose and mouth to be kissed, my hands began to tremble—a reaction which nothing had ever before been able to arouse in me.

We went back to the lobby, and I said to her, "Sit here a minute."

Obediently she sat down in one of the hundred armchairs. I asked the night porter for another form, filled it out, and took a second room on another floor. She saw the key in my hand, as I came back to her.

"What's that?" she asked.

"A key."

"For our room?"

"No. My room."

"But before, you . . ."

"I know, I know. We took a double room. You're going to sleep in that, just you. And I in this."

She gazed at me, as though I had told her the most startling news in the world. While she was so amazed, her eyes took on a deep violet shade. There were moments when I seriously believed she could change the color of her eyes at will. This much is sure, that her eyes had four or five distinct colors. If I had to testify under oath before a court, I could not say what color her eyes were. Even though I don't believe anyone ever looked so long and so often into a woman's eyes as I did into hers. To tell the truth, I still cannot think of her as a human being. The penetrating, lightning-quick shock which, between Milan and Genoa, had hit me like a sudden and unexpected infection—that shock affected me so that I could never think of her as a normal earthly being, no matter how persistently

I tried to discover just those human traits in her. This phrase tortured me constantly: "I did not fall in love with her, but she forced me to fall in love with her." By forbidden perverse arts, just as in the old fairy tales women gave magic potions, love philters, to the men they desired.

Looking at the key in my hand, she asked very softly, "You don't want to sleep in the same room with me even for this half night until tomorrow morning?"

"No."

As I spoke that "no," I felt that the life impulse was speaking in me. The fear of death. The reader of these notes will not laugh at me for this—he will see that I was right. Not as if I believed that—if we were together —she would kill me during the night for no other reason than the few lire and dollars I had in my pocket. I wasn't afraid of that. But I felt that if I went to sleep alone in a hotel room now, it would be my last opportunity to be alone with myself. To attempt, hopelessly, to forget, to sleep off, to vomit up the whole suddenly-caught insanity. The thought—no, the certainty —pursued me that every minute I spent with this girl would be a minute in a slow murder, stretched out over months, perhaps over years. Even the short while I had spent with her since this afternoon, when she boarded the train at Lausanne, represented the first few hours in a slow process of murder.

These few hours would not have been so unspeakably joyful-painful had they not meant the beginning of destruction because of a woman. It must have been an obsession—or perhaps a presentiment?—but that day I felt I was faced with something like the fate of those insects, who, by the inscrutable will of God, must pay with death for their life's single moment of love. I was thinking of the famous winged red ants, whose females fly upward with swarms of their males, make love high in the air, and afterward let their mates fall down dead. A French scholar wrote about them: in the sunset, like a shower of gold, a million dead lovers slowly fall . . .

"No," I returned, in answer to her proposal to spend the night with me, and walked toward the elevator. I must have seemed ridiculous, with my mournful steps.

She ran after me.

She said gently, "Let me sleep in your room. I swear it's not for *that*."

"No," I said. I could feel the blood drain from my cheeks.

She got in the elevator with me. Her room was two floors above mine. When I got out, she unexpectedly got out, too.

"Your room is two floors up," I said hoarsely.

"I know," she said, and began to cry almost soundlessly, softly, like a child whom someone has hurt deeply. She pulled out a laughably small handkerchief and blew her nose in it. The elevator man took the lift down. In the long corridor, only a third of the lights were burning, with a sickly yellow light. I looked at my key. 325. Then I read the number on a door. I had a long way to go to 325. She was crying so silently that, before I started on my way, I turned, thinking she had disappeared, had run on tiptoe over the thick carpet. No. She stood where she had stood before, in front of the elevator, and wept silently into that laughably small handkerchief. I left her there, went on my way down the long corridor in the direction of number 325, and felt that I had been cruel, not to her, but only to myself. I stopped in front of the door to 325, but I did not look back, because I was certain she was still standing there. I went into the little room and slammed the door unnecessarily loud. Inside I turned the key twice, also unnecessarily loud.

Up to then I had never done a thing like that—or anything resembling it—to any woman.

CHAPTER FOUR

A FEW WORDS about myself. First of all, I am by no means an exciting person. I am an unimportant, skillful, respectable, and experienced journalist. I have no real friends, because in Budapest I lived a rather dour, solitary bachelor existence. My permanent home was a cheap room in the Hotel Metropole. I got up late, went without breakfast, ate lunch in some little restaurant, and after lunch played cards for two or three hours with my colleagues in the Otthon Journalists' Club. In the afternoon and night I worked in the editorial room, or rambled about the city on some reporting job. In the evening, I hung around in the wings of one or another of the operetta theaters, because I also wrote a weekly column of theater gossip.

I had drifted from the mountain region of north Hungary to riotous Budapest, which in those days believed it was the center of the world. My father, who died when I was a child, had a hotel in the mountain region. My mother and sister carried on the business. I inherited a portion of my father's estate; and later I inherited something from my mother, too. At that time you could live on a capital as small as the one that had been left me. My mother and sister remained in the hotel in the provinces, but they sent me to Budapest to be educated. I went to the Protestant High School and lived with a good man, named Szinten, who was sexton of the Protestant church of which the school was a part. My mother and sister wanted me to be a lawyer. But I left law school at eighteen to become a journalist. At nineteen I was writing short stories that were later translated into German and French, for Viennese and Parisian magazines. I never got any further. Every evening I spent several hours in the wings of some theater, but I never wanted to try writing a play myself. I was in part too modest, in part too timid, for work of such scope.

I was drafted late in the first great war. I was attached as assistant to an Austrian captain named Harbaur. He was a decent fellow. We published a Hungarian newspaper in Kovel, Russia, for the northern army. Later, when Captain Harbaur was transferred to Headquarters Press Service, he took me with him. So I played little active part with sword and gun in the great, four-year-long bloodshed. After the war, as before it, my social life was carried on among my own sort, moderately successful journalists. My so-called love life was confined to chorus girls and very unimportant second-rate actresses.

Love? Once, just once, I experienced something like it, and then I immediately got married. I married one of these second-rate actresses—she had a pretty face, was much taller than I, and a serious girl. But after four months we were divorced. It was my fault. The poor girl set up our little home hopefully, full of joyful expectation at being free of the Bohemian life at last, and able to throw herself into a respectable family existence, and perhaps even into repeated motherhood. But just then—for the first and last time in my life—I got in with a card playing crowd, lost, fell into debt, was fired from my job, began to drink, and didn't dare come home for days at a time. No wonder my wife left me. A nasty story. I don't like to think about it.

After our divorce, my wife gave up her hopes of family life, joined a dance troupe, and danced her way through the Near and then the Far East. Faithfully, she sent me picture postcards with loving messages from Greece, Turkey, and Egypt, and afterward from the islands of east Asia. Those islands which in this war are beginning to be mentioned so frequently in the articles of English experts on naval strategy. The last card I received from her was from Surabaya. In it she told me she had married the Dutch captain of a freighter, and that they would both come to see me. It was one of the few truly moving evenings of my life when one day Irma actually appeared in my room in Budapest with her husband, the Dutch captain, an elderly, very serious gentleman. They had really come from east Asia to Budapest to see Irma's old mother, but once they were there, Irma presented her first husband, myself, to the captain. Irma was much more beautiful than before, and they both seemed so happy that for some hours afterward I envied the captain.

I left Budapest three or four years before the new war broke out. At the time, I was working on an evening paper where I had to begin work at eight in the morning. It was torture for me to have to get up at six-thirty, accustomed as I was to going to bed at three or four in the morning. I had to get up at six-thirty because the Hotel Metropole, where I lived, was a long distance from the newspaper office. I tormented myself for about six months before I discovered that there was a neat, well-kept little hotel, the Bristol, just across from the editorial offices, only a minute away.

I left my dear, familiar room in the Metropole, and moved over to the Bristol, so that I could sleep an extra hour every day. After my first night at the Bristol, the editor-in-chief of the newspaper called me in at nine in the morning and told me that they had to cut down expenses and were, therefore, letting six employees go, me among them. "By chance" all six of these journalists were Jewish. So I finally left Budapest, with a very bad taste in my mouth. Half my small capital was in Switzerland, the other half in New York. In any case, I could not have stayed in Budapest much longer, because if it had become known that I had money abroad, they would have thrown me in jail for five years.

I lived in Nice, in Venice. In summer in Geneva. I made it a principle to live in a cheap room in an expensive hotel. So in all three places I lived in holes in the attic, but walked through glittering halls to eat in the near-by bistros.

There was one excellent newspaper in Nice—perhaps it's still there—*L'Eclaireur de Nice*. I can remember the exact date; it was on February 3, 1939, at nine in the morning that—lying in bed next to the open window in the warm sunshine—I read in this paper that all was up with Europe. It was a clever, wicked, typically French political article whose logic was crystal clear. I was terrified. I read it again. Even here in the sweet, lighthearted atmosphere of the Riviera, there had for a long time now been some sense of what the article described. But this article spoke out the whole cruel truth. I dressed, stuck my passport into my pocket, and went to the American consulate to ask for a passport to the United States.

"Why do you want to go to America?" the consul asked me.

"I'd like to see the New York World's Fair," I told him.

Nice was full of posters of the New York World's Fair. I got the visa at once. That's why I remember the date, February 3, 1939. But when spring came, I didn't go to America, but to Switzerland, to Geneva. I spent the summer and autumn there. The autumn mostly close to the radio, like thousands of other foreigners in Geneva. There were some who even brought their little portable radios into the restaurants with them. That remains an unforgettable memory of Geneva— those frightened refugees, dining in the cheap beer houses, with the little portable radios on the center of their tables. Geneva was already full of refugees then. The hotels were overflowing with Germans, Poles, Austrians, Hungarians; and Switzerland didn't like them much. Didn't like them at all. Visitors' permits were extended for a few weeks, only with the greatest difficulty and to the accompaniment of increasingly sharp threats. More and more bewildered Jews sat perplexedly in the coffeehouses. University professors, famous writers, big industrialists, actors.

By November I began to be very nervous and to suffer from insomnia. Everyone was saying that either the German or French army would march into Switzerland, and then everything would be over for us "visitors." Long lines of people stood in the corridors of the American consulate, but the consul gave none of them visas. The consul didn't like them, either. He didn't like them at all. I cling stubbornly to the conviction that no consul likes anyone. Whether foreigners or his own countrymen. I know I am being unjust. There are exceptions. There are certainly many hundreds of consuls who are as kind as Saint Francis of Assisi, but of the uncountable number of consuls with whom I've had to deal in my life, I've never found one who liked the person just then standing in front of his office desk.

My visa was valid until February 3, 1940. On Christmas Eve, 1939, after dinner, I went to a café where ten or twelve Hungarian emigrants gathered at a big table. At the next table a drunken German Jew was explaining to his companions very loudly and convincingly that Switzerland was a mousetrap from which one could still escape into Italy. But if the Italians got into the war, too, the mousetrap would snap shut for good. Then no foreigner could get out of there, not one. That same night, at home in bed, I figured out coolly and unemotionally that if I transferred the Swiss part of my small capital to New York, too, with careful handling my money would hold out for four years—with a little hunger, perhaps six years. Next morning I transferred my money from Switzerland to the Guaranty Trust in New York; and on December 31, I started on the trip I have described above, by way of Milan and Genoa, to New York.

My appearance? I haven't a single gray hair yet. I refer you to the red-haired girl who said that I didn't look fifty-two. As a matter of fact, I look five or six years younger. As they say here, my face is a "nice" face. Not effeminate and not very masculine either, particularly since I had my little mustache shaved off. My face, my expression which is always somewhat sad, is distinctly Slavic in type. My sister looks like me, and we often used to talk about how our forefathers, Jews who emigrated to north Hungary from Russia a hundred and fifty years ago, brought strong traces of some Russian alliance with them. Why wasn't it possible that the father of one of our ancestors was a Russian country lad who, near some ghetto, fell in love with a pretty Jewish girl, and made her a mother without even being able to consider marriage—in the empire of the czars in the eighteenth century.

I am not a striking sight. No one looks at me when I come into a restaurant, or bar, or theater. I think I would have to walk into a New York night club in yellow trousers, scarlet-red dinner jacket, and a green tie before a woman would notice me. The way I ordinarily look and dress no one is particularly curious about me. I speak in a soft voice, unobtrusively. I am five foot seven, and weigh 153 pounds.

No more average man—both physically and spiritually—ever existed. Why did she choose just me, just me, *just me,* to kill?

CHAPTER FIVE

O N THE morning of the second day the sun shone so hot on the bar at the bow of the S.S. *Rex* that it was hard for us to believe the calendar, which said it was January 2. The ship had sailed from Genoa on New Year's Day, and now lay in Naples Harbor, where it usually picked up the last European passengers. The huge bar on the top deck was empty. I sat near the open door at a small table on which the south Italian sun was shining. I was drinking a cup of *café expresso*. The—I don't know how many cups it was since breakfast.

I had slept very well the first night on shipboard. The sense of escape from worried, frightened Europe was doubly sweet in the lovely morning sunshine, after such a good sleep—after all those dark, icy mornings in Geneva, after all those restless nights. One discovers with astonishment that there is still such unexpected happiness in the world, such fresh sweet moments as this beginning of a new life. In a few hours the ship will set out toward the West. Then there will be only the open sea, the wind, the sky—until we reach America. In the past few years, America has been to us the "hundred per cent" fairyland. Better to be a beggar in America, people think—and say—than a king in

Europe. All lives have a new beginning in America. Even the most hopeless.

Suddenly, unexpectedly, Edith was standing beside my table. Yesterday we boarded the ship together. But this morning, here at this table glistening in the sunshine, I must confess I had forgotten her for a few minutes in the great American dream. And I can also confess that, from that day to this, it was the only short span of time for which I forgot she was in the world. Never since then, not for a minute.

She gazed at me reproachfully. "I've been looking all over for you. Where have you been hiding?"

She was so direct and so possessive that I was amazed. What was this? The day before yesterday I didn't know she existed, and today she was acting as if I were her property.

She drank a glass of the good, strong Italian coffee, too. Then we went out into the sun together, to the ship's bow, where there was no one but us. A sharp wind was blowing. Edith put her arm through mine. She was looking at me, and I pressed her to me, and was happy. I kissed her lovely full lips for a long time. She clutched the back of my head, sank her hand deep into my hair, and pressed my head down on her mouth. I know all these are commonplace things, and happen to every man. But looking back on this portion of my life, that banal moment seems to me as important a point in my biography as the moment in Napoleon's life when he placed the imperial crown on his head in the Cathedral of Notre Dame de Paris.

Two elderly men appeared in the open door of the bar.

"Hello, Edith!" one shouted gaily.

The other lifted his arm to her in greeting. They had both boarded the ship today, here in Naples.

"Petrovitch!" Edith cried, and turned to me to explain, "Mr. Petrovitch and Mr. Bauer . . . the Café Elysée . . . the Café Monaco . . ."

Both of these fine-sounding names were the names of very low Budapest night clubs.

"Don't introduce me," I mumbled out of the corner of my mouth to Edith, and sneaked away while she was laughingly embracing the night-club owners.

Mr. Petrovitch and Mr. Bauer didn't pay much attention to me. Edith told me later that she had worked for them both for several months as a dancer. One of the gentlemen—Mr. Petrovitch—in delight at seeing her again, smacked her a couple of times on the behind. I only mention this to show how far the poisoning process had already gone in me—but at that moment I had the feeling I was a husband watching a strange man slap his wife on the buttocks, and permitting it without protest. I walked slowly away from them, but I had already caught enough to know that the two brothelkeepers were going to America, and were going to open a night spot with dancing, Hungarian food and drinks, a Hungarian band—and Hungarian girls. In the course of their conversation, they made various vulgar comments which made it clear that in their world Edith had actually been famous because she was a virgin. I escaped down a little stairway, discovered at just the right moment—I had no idea where it led—as they were snickeringly explaining to Edith that she wouldn't be a real dancer or a really pretty girl until she finally lost her virginity. At that moment, to be exact, I felt like a brother who listens to two old brothelkeepers giving his sister that kind of advice, and permits them to do it.

I had run down the narrow little stairs, and found myself in a kind of library, where a bespectacled old lady inquired helpfully what book I wanted. But before I could answer, Edith appeared beside me, grabbed my arm, and led me out into the open, on deck.

"Are you angry at me?"

"Why should I be?"

"On account of those two men."

"Now, really!"

"I can't help their being so vulgar. Poor things, they're homeless, too, because Bauer is a Jew, and Petrovitch once kicked a drunken Nazi out of his joint. Don't be angry."

She stroked my face. That was one of her most extraordinary characteristics: she knew instinctively what cure to prescribe. Actually, the stroking meant nothing. But at the moment it did me good. Like a nice little decoration to a soldier. When a woman begins to feel that a man is in her power, no medical genius can figure out so precisely when and what medicine and how much of it should be given, as a woman's instinct.

Well then, a twenty-one-year-old girl pats a fifty-two-year-old man just as she would a strange little dog in an elevator. And just this transforms an unpleasant moment in the life of the fifty-two-year-old into a pleasant one. What does it mean? Is it the infallibility of the female instinct, of which we've been told a million times over, or our less willingly admitted masculine inferiority?

Passengers were still coming up the gangplank onto the ship. Among the very last I found someone I knew, too. A young man from Budapest, Pali Maybaum. Back home, he was a screen writer. Everybody knew that, even though he had never written a single movie. But he was very clever and talented about the movies—in conversation at night in a café. For decades, this talent had been sufficient for an artistic career in Budapest. We had painters who, instead of painting, talked about painting in cafés, so well and in such a revolutionary manner that they enjoyed great artistic reputations among the younger painters. We had young doctors who operated in the coffeehouses with words, writers who recited the plots of novels in coffeehouses—better than the works of others which appeared in print. We had coffeehouse Shakespearean actors. The best Hamlet I ever heard was not on the stage, but in the Café Seyffert in Budapest at four in the morning. And even so, people were somehow sure that Pali Maybaum was talented. I was glad when he came on board, because I felt he was now moving in the right direction. He had started for Hollywood, for the one place where he belonged. He was a tall young man, broad-shouldered, narrow-hipped, brown-haired. In spite of his big nose and puffy lips, he was decidedly handsome. He looked more like a movie actor than a writer. He must have been about twenty-six or twenty-seven, I'm not quite certain. Once in Budapest, he told me he was twenty-seven, but a few days later he forgot, and told some other people in my presence that he was thirty-one. I think this characterizes Pali, even if not completely.

He greeted me impetuously. Threw his arms around me, kissed me—couldn't believe I was really here, that I was going to America, too. He was full of good spirits and pure youthful joy.

On the shore below, a girl shouted to him, "Pali! Pali!"

Pali blew her a kiss. The girl was holding a handkerchief in her hand, and alternately waving and wiping her eyes with it. But Pali concentrated entirely on me. He threw his arms around me and shook my hand.

"My, what a coincidence! This is a surprise!"

From below, the girl shouted up sadly, reproachfully, "Pali! Pali!"

Instead of looking down toward the shore, Pali stared at Edith so intently that I was forced to introduce them, which I did not wish to do. Pali is an attractive young man, and it was common knowledge that he had no scruples. I saw that Pali liked the girl. I didn't notice anything about Edith, although, as it turned out later, she liked Pali even more than he did her. The German tanks were already beginning the destruction of Europe. France was preparing its life-and-death struggle, Russia was awake and sharpening her weapons, the whole world was secretly on fire, even though the fire had not yet blazed to the skies—and I was trying with profound seriousness to discover whether Pali didn't like Edith somewhat more than was necessary.

I don't want to make myself ridiculous in retrospect, but I am setting this down with the idea that perhaps someday a psychiatrist may read these notes of mine with objective interest. Don't misunderstand me. I don't consider that my way of thinking at the time was abnormal. I believed, and still believe, that the German tanks and the Maginot Line were the abnormalities. I was not ashamed, and will never be ashamed, that the simple expressions of the suffering human soul were more important to me than all political history. Once, when I was still very young and revolutionary, I pompously explained—in a coffeehouse, of course—that the history of mankind was no credit to God. Later, when I learned to like the Russian writers, particularly Dostoevsky, I added to this—again in a coffeehouse—that the human soul, the soul of every single individual, was God's greatest pride. He is not God because He created the oceans and the stars, but, to me, He is God because He shaped the human soul as it is. In the eyes of a serious philosopher, these might seem extravagantly youthful phrases, but as for me, I am not afraid even now to admit that I believed in them. Now, when the only principle that guides my writing is not to lie, I confess that my nervous torment on account of a girl did not appear at all ridiculous or shameful to me, compared to my concern over Europe's tragedy—and for a time was even more painful to me than the news about the *blitz*.

"Pali! Pali!" the girl with the handkerchief shouted from below.

"For God's sake," I said to the boy, "speak to her, or wave. The girl's crying. Is she your girl?"

"Yes," Pali said.

He blew kisses to her. The poor girl began to cry violently into her handkerchief.

"My fiancée," Pali said to us, as if he were apologizing for the girl sobbing on the shore.

"Ella!" he called down to her. "Don't cry! I love you! I love you!"

Ella smiled behind her handkerchief, and went on crying.

"Poor little girl," Pali said. "She came this far with me from Budapest. It'll be hard for her to take the long trip back alone."

"Go on, say something nice to her," Edith said to Pali.

"That's all I've been doing for two days and two nights," Pali answered.

"But can't you see how she's crying?"

Pali smiled meaningfully.

"You have no idea how nice I've been to her for

forty-eight consecutive hours. But if that's what you want . . ."

He cupped his hands over his mouth and called loudly down to the girl.

"I'll love you for ever and ever, I swear, I swear, I swear!"

He said it in a tremulous voice, the way certain actors speak that kind of line. Edith and the girl on the pier were visibly moved by this speech. But for my part, even today, I don't know whether his voice really trembled or whether it was a mock tremolo. Pali often seemed to be acting a part.

He turned to Edith.

"Now, are you pleased with me?"

A general waving began as the ship made ready to sail. Ella and Pali waved madly to each other. I stood apart with Edith, leaving the rail to those people who were being waved at from the shore.

"Sad that they have to separate just now," Edith said, looking at Pali's fiancée. "Two such lovely young people. And they're being separated just now, when . . . we two . . ."

I looked at her in amazement. This was something new, this sentimental tone from her.

"Just now," she said, "when we have found each other."

The ship began to move. Edith took my arm and led me to the other side, where you could look out over the open sea.

"Who's the handsome young man?" she asked on the way.

"Movie writer," I answered shortly, almost angrily. The way she put the question—and that barely audible melody of real female interest I thought I caught in it—disturbed me.

CHAPTER SIX

T HE THREE of us ate at the same table. From time to time I wove into the conversation the fact that Pali had a fiancée—and achieved just the opposite effect from what I intended. I noticed that Edith stared at him intently and uninterruptedly. Just the way she had stared at me the day before yesterday on the train. Before she knew me.

Once when I mentioned the word "fiancée," Pali screwed up his mouth and made a contemptuous gesture. Edith spoke sharply.

"What does *that* mean? Isn't she your fiancée?"

"Oh, yes."

"Then why didn't you take her along to America?"

I broke in nervously, "Drop it, Edith. It's his business. We'd better not ask him about it."

Edith repeated quietly, "Why didn't you take her along to America?"

"Because I haven't very much money," Pali said.

"Will you send for her when you make money?"

Pali answered with deep conviction.

"No."

Edith went on with her questioning.

"Will you go back to her?"

"Never," Pali said quietly, with a nasty smile and a

shrug of the shoulders. Edith's hand lay on the table. Pali, still with the same nasty smile on his face, laid his hand quietly on Edith's, and Edith did not draw her hand away. Even after this unpleasant little dialogue she didn't stop staring at the fellow. Not only wasn't she indignant, but she looked on him as a hero. Today I know why he appealed to her so much even then. Because she felt he was of the same stuff as she—a murderer. That the screen writer was a murderer of women and she a murderer of men made no difference. Apparently, murderers recognize and like each other.

After lunch, as we went up the steps, Edith hurried ahead. Pali used the opportunity to nudge me in the ribs.

"Who's the kitten with the nice legs?"

"I don't know," I whispered. "The first time I saw her was in the train the day before yesterday."

I wanted to disparage her, belittle her in his eyes, so he would lose interest in her. Slowly but surely in those days I was beginning to turn into an ass.

"She has absolutely even legs," Pali said. "Very rare. Not bowed and not knock-kneed."

He said this fairly loud. Undoubtedly so that the girl, who was going up the steps in front of us, would hear it. Then he went into his cabin. I caught up with Edith, and we sat down to coffee.

"Attractive fellow," Edith said.

"Really? Do you like that vulgar manner?"

"No."

"Or the way he treats his fiancée?"

"No."

"Then what's so attractive about him?"

Edith shrugged her shoulders.

"I'm enchanted by him."

"Anyone can see," I said, with open bitterness, "that you come from the world of the Café Elysée and Café Monaco. What kind of exaggeration is that, 'I'm enchanted by him'? Why?"

"Because he's different. Not commonplace."

Hmm, I thought, so this girl is stupid besides. Now I'm absolutely sure she's stupid. I was chilled and furious, but I said nothing. We went to our own cabins for our afternoon nap. I couldn't fall asleep. The boat was tossing more violently than yesterday, and besides I was more tense. I was restless. We had made an appointment for five o'clock in the bar, but at four-thirty I began to look for her. First in her cabin, then in all the places we had so far discovered on the ship. I couldn't find her anywhere. Bar, library, writing room, lounge— nowhere. It began to grow dark. From the bar I went to the bow of the ship. The weather was mild, but even so, the ship was pitching furiously. The point of the bow sank down to the water, then rose majestically to the clouds. Too many lights were burning. Neutral Italian ships were much too brightly lighted. Two solemn men were standing under a light. Mr. W., the well-known Zionist leader, and Mr. B., one of the highest officials in the British Embassy in Washington. It was whispered about the ship that, somewhere in the distance, a British destroyer was accompanying our Italian ship for his protection. I never saw the destroyer, but, like the rest of the passengers, I was proud of it. The Zionist leader and the British diplomat went into the bar, where ladies were waiting for them. For a moment I thought about them with bitter envy. I envied them their troubles. The new Palestinian homeland of the exiled Jews was the problem of one, the fate of the British Empire, of the other. Neither was curious about what I was curious about—where a red-haired girl was keeping herself and with whom. I felt that I was more torn by this trouble of mine than the gentlemen by their great historic troubles. They sat down with the ladies and began their bridge game. Edith was—nowhere. I walked the length of the ship along the upper deck, under the lifeboats, where it smelled of oil and tar and smoke, then back again to the lounge. The afternoon concert had already begun. I noticed that I was walking excitedly. I was rushing, lurching about. Why?

Half aloud I said to myself, "Walk quietly. Walk slowly. No reason to get upset." And at the same time I slowed my pace to a walk.

Then I saw them, in the constantly increasing but still warm wind, standing in a corner, very close together. They were laughing. Pali was standing with his back to me. He did not see me. He was kissing Edith, a long kiss. Somehow I had the feeling that this might be the tenth kiss. I could see it had all happened with the girl's consent, even encouragement. She pressed her hand on the back of the boy's head, into his hair, just as she had in my hair this morning, and pulled his head toward her. Slowly I approached them. What drove me crazy was that the girl stood facing me, saw me, and did not stop. She simply took no notice of me. Not a single muscle of her face changed. I saw plainly that she saw me, that she was looking directly at me. "Tremendous presence of mind." I caught myself not only thinking it, but saying it half aloud. She went on kissing the boy and looking at me. My lips moved again: "Tremendous presence of mind."

Out of the confusion of the following minutes I only remember clearly that I hit Pali. I hit his mouth with my fist. I hit him blindly in the face, without aiming, but I hit the mouth with which he had sinned. Sinned? I told you I had become an ass.

The girl yelled at me.

"Fool!"

"Yes," I said half unconsciously.

"Dangerous fool!"

She was furious. She rushed away, ran from there under the lifeboats. She disappeared behind a door. I turned and went back to the bar. I don't remember any more whether Pali stayed there or went away. I sat down on one of the high stools at the bar and ordered a double cognac. My heart was pounding so hard that I began to take my pulse. It was beating terribly quickly and irregularly. I looked at the Zionist leader and the British diplomat, hating them both because they were examining the cards in their hands with great concern, engrossed in some bridge problem or other. They looked as if, at the moment, life was hurting them as much as it was me. I gulped down the cognac, and reeled to my cabin to try to straighten out all the madness, the confusion, in my mind. After these last few days, I felt I must cleanse my brain and ventilate it. Even now I don't understand everything that had happened to me in those few days. That's exactly why I'm writing it down. I'm writing it down for those who believe that everything has a reason. That there's an explanation for everything. Who believe that dangerous women are remarkably beautiful, or exciting, or mysterious. That the male victim is a type bad women recognize and select the instant they see one. I'm writing it down for those who believe that men are able to decide how things shall happen. I'm writing it for those to whom you can't explain that some things are inexplicable.

As I entered my cabin, I was startled to see that Edith was lying, fully dressed, on my bed, crying. It was the first time she had been in my cabin. A long silence. Then—a real fool—I asked:

"Why did you kiss that fellow?"

She answered, crying, "For you to see. I saw you coming. Couldn't you tell I saw you?"

"Yes, I could tell."

"That's when I let him kiss me."

"For the tenth time," said the fool.

"For the first time," lied the girl.

"For the twentieth time," said I.

"For the first time," she repeated stubbornly.

Blackly, furiously, she looked at me.

"I wanted to make you jealous. I wanted to make you lose your head. You icicle. You coward, you. What are you afraid of? Because you read that in America they sentence any man who's dragged into court by a girl? You ought to be ashamed to be so frightened of a girl like me."

"Why were you in such a hurry about it?" I asked. "Why didn't you wait a few days? It's only a couple of hours since you met that boy. Did it have to happen right away? Why?"

"I couldn't stand your caution any longer. Separate rooms in the hotel. Separate cabins on the boat. A cautious kiss in the morning, in the sunshine, in public. I couldn't stand it any longer. I won't stand it. I had to be finished with it. Now I've put it behind me. Now you're standing there all broken up. Just half the size you were this morning. That's what I wanted."

Stubbornly I persisted in my question.

"But why so quickly? Why right away?"

Her eyes shone.

"Because he attracts me."

I looked at her as though she were out of her mind. She added hastily, "I needed it . . . because with a man like you I lose my self-confidence."

"Am I supposed to get used to it?" I asked bitterly. She smiled at me innocently through her tears, like a two-year-old child. What is this? Nymphomania, of which she herself doesn't know? No. So far there's been no sign of it.

She saw the tortured expression on my face.

"I'm not speaking logically, am I?" she said.

I didn't answer. I only knew I must leave the ship immediately, immediately, if I still hoped to save myself belatedly from this witch. And yet—how lucky that you couldn't leave a ship in the middle of the ocean.

She wiped her tears and reached out her hand to me.

"Come, lie down beside me, and we'll be quiet for a long time together."

I lay down beside her, fully dressed. On the narrow bed, I had to squeeze very close to her. She lay on the side next to the wall. I listened to her quiet, slow breathing for a long time. She was staring up at the ceiling like a person who is thinking very intently about a problem. I thought enviously again of the Zionist leader and the British diplomat—how fortunate they were not to know this girl and to be able to think about quite different things. My face, against which hers was pressed, was red hot.

"Have you a temperature?" she asked gently, like a mother.

"I don't know."

"Have you a thermometer?"

"Yes."

"In your bag?"

"Yes."

"Don't move," she said. "Just lie there quietly. I'll get it."

She stood up and stepped carefully over me. As I lay there on my back, I saw her white thighs above her stockings for the first time. If only I knew everything as surely as I know today that she took those steps for that very reason!

She found the thermometer in my bag as quickly as if she had packed it. She was diabolically clever about things like that. Found everything, could open everything. She discovered instantly what was wrong with anything that broke, whether it was the water faucet, a door handle, radio, alarm clock, fountain pen—anything.

She sat down on the edge of the bed. Stuck the thermometer in my mouth. We waited the required number of minutes. The ship was rocking us with gentle, even rhythm now. I looked at her, stupidly and unhappily, with the thermometer protruding from my closed mouth. She took it out and looked at it with the expert glance of a nurse.

"You have fever," she said.

I looked at the thermometer.

"I've had that much every afternoon for several years," I said.

"Do you cough?"

"No."

She pressed my tongue down with the handle of a spoon and looked down my throat. She unbuttoned the shirt over my chest, pressed her ear against me, and listened to my lungs and my heart—all this just so her thick red hair would brush my nose and I would smell that sharp, provocative odor.

"The trouble is here," she said, and with that smile

of a two-year-old child, she laid her warm, soft hand on my heart.

"My heart? I've never had a bit of trouble with it."

"Not your trouble," she said. "My trouble."

"How so?"

"I'm in love with you," she said. "By the way, what's your name?"

It was apparent that this "What's your name" was a joke, and a tasteless one at that. Not even well carried out, because it didn't sound like a real question. I didn't answer, of course, only smiled. But I must confess—and let's not for a moment forget that I was fifty-two—that, after all that had happened between us since the day before yesterday, the question, quite literally, hurt me. If that was her aim, she hit it the way a good sharpshooter hits a target, right in the middle.

I only saw Pali once again before we reached American waters. It was the next day at noon. In the morning Edith came out with the fact that Pali was miserable, and willing to do anything, if only, for God's sake, I wouldn't be angry at him.

"I'm not angry at him," I said.

"Would you shake hands with him if he came to you?"

"No."

"How long are you going to be angry at him?"

"I've told you already, I'm not angry."

"Are you angry at me?"

"Yes."

"Then why did you shake hands with me?"

"That," I said, "is one of those eternal and insoluble questions which for thousands of years not even the wisest men have been able to answer."

We ate at two separate tables. Edith and I sat at yesterday's table. Pali sat alone at a tiny table next to the wall. He must have been pretty embarrassed, because he changed his seat twice so as not to have to look at us.

In the evening, Edith showed me a note. Pali had written her that he was dreadfully seasick. He had to stay in bed, and the doctor was taking care of him. I thought he was playing a comedy for my benefit. But as it turned out, he really was sick, like half the other passengers. Neither Edith nor I was sick. It's an old superstition of mine that a person who's very occupied with something has no time to be sick. In spite of the Mediterranean's good reputation, it was a nasty January. In every respect. The United Press dispatches from Europe, pinned up near the purser's office, were frightfully bad, too. Every time I stood there reading them, I shivered, thinking by what a hair's breadth I had escaped—and from what!

Edith was looking at me, the note in her hand.

"Someone really ought to visit the poor thing."

I didn't answer.

"Should I go down for a minute? Just to see if he needs anything?"

"So far as I know," I said, "seasickness isn't catching. You can safely visit a person who's seasick."

(The next instant I was ashamed of my answer.) Edith tore up the note.

"I'm not going down to him," she said, and I felt that she meant it as a favor to me.

"For God's sake," I said angrily, "don't make any sacrifices. Do what you like."

She didn't go down to him. Or, rather, to this day I don't know whether she went down to him or not. At first I had an impulse to spy on her, but when she disappeared down the corridor I didn't follow. For a man who lives by his brains, it is shocking bankruptcy to spend hours—as war is breaking out—racking those brains over whether a certain Edith is going to a certain cabin or not. I knew that all Europe had gone mad. And here was I, a little man on a boat in the middle of the ocean . . . being driven crazy by something entirely different from Europe's millions . . . by a trifle so unimportant that any other man would have given up with a sigh, freed himself of it with money, or settled the matter in bed—rolling in the hay a night or two, laughing with a laughing woman. To be driven crazy by this, just now, when history was literally beginning to burn . . . didn't this show an extraordinarily low intellectual level? No, it only showed that some poison, some infection, had taken root in me, and was destroying me. I had certainly been poisoned by the girl—foolish as that may sound. Up to the time I was fifty-two, I was normal and drab. I shared the viewpoint of hundreds of thousands of average middle-European men on the woman question, a viewpoint which lay somewhere between the West and the East, halfway between the French cult of love and the Oriental idea that a man can buy female flesh by the pound. Women interested me less than they did other men. Only when nature absolutely demanded it. No more and no less. I had run away from so-called love, particularly since my short marriage and divorce. Even though running away was not always simple, because women sense this impulse toward flight in a man, and it attracts them more than anything else.

The only thought that consoled me was that this voyage would eventually end. And America is breathtakingly big, thank God. Never, never again will I so much as see her. Why should a hussy like this suddenly interest me now? Just because Europe has thrown me out, and I, a lonesome bachelor, have become even more lonesome among so many strangers? That can't be true. God knows, up to now I've only been interested in my profession. And even now that's all that interests me. A profession into which a man can escape, which he can love.

I was filled with enthusiasm, thinking of the newspaper profession. Yes . . . the *New York Times'* organization, its editorial offices, its building, its presses, its machines—*that* interested me. I had heard they were glad to show it all to foreign journalists. I would go through their building ten times, twenty times, and I'd make a thousand notes.

And in New York I would collect the facts about the war and current history from the uncensored press! I

would have a hundred thousand clippings. All classi-
fied. Catalogues! Cabinets, drawers! Boxes! For how
many articles and books I would have assembled mate-
rial by the end of the war! And—although I spoke English—I would perfect my knowledge of the language.
That's what there was to do! Organize a pro-American
news bureau for postwar Europe—not gaze at a red-
haired girl . . . with the scent of her hair in my nose
. . . with her hot fingers on my naked chest . . . No!
But to lay the foundation for a great agency . . .
feeding all Europe with liberal pro-American articles
. . . an agency which immediately after the war would
begin sending articles—to Germany from the German
émigrés, to Paris from the French, to Budapest from
the Hungarians, to Athens from the Greeks, and to all
the others . . . build up a great organization . . .
begin right away . . . gradually select the best men,
to think about that . . . right away . . . only about
that . . .

But not to lie, hot with fever, on a ship's bed, with
my face pressed against the face of a strange girl . . .
or standing at the bow of the ship, to kiss that girl on
the mouth like any excited, idiotic stripling . . . and
in free America to be the slave of a good-for-nothing
girl who is not beautiful, not interesting, not intelligent, not unusual, but who attracts Pali Maybaum and
everyone else, and—I watched it—the waiters and the
bartenders, and the captain, and the ship's doctor, and
all the men at all the surrounding tables . . . and
about whom I have the manic conviction that she loves

me better than anyone else in the world, and that she will only express and satisfy this love of hers by killing me. Surely, an obsession. But that—whether she knows it or not—she is going to kill me, and has the ability and power to do so, there is no doubt.

There's no use pretending. I was afraid.

CHAPTER SEVEN

A SMALL PIECE of paper appeared on the black bulletin board where the news was regularly posted for the passengers. It contained the information that the *Rex* would stop at two unscheduled places on its way to America—Lisbon, and Horta in the Azores. For the past two weeks, the Lisbon clipper had canceled its flights because of bad weather. A group of travelers, mostly Americans, all of whom had wanted to be home in time for Christmas, were stuck in Lisbon and in the Azores. The weather forecast continued bad, so this marooned group had arranged at great expense to have the *Rex,* which was on its way to America, stop for them. This would make our trip two days longer. Not good news. I had to be shut in with her two days longer.

One morning when I woke, the ship had stopped. I pushed the curtain back from the porthole. It was raining. Through the veil of rain I could see the shore and houses in the distance. The steward brought my breakfast.

"Lisbon," he said, putting down the tray. "We'll be here until noon. Do you know Lisbon?"

"No."

"Never been there?"

"Never."

"A rather sad little town," he said. "But they're not going to get into this war, the Portuguese. They've got a sensible dictator. Not like us Italians."

When I went up on deck the rain was dropping sadly from dark, gray clouds. We were anchored fairly far away from provincial-looking Lisbon. Gazing around the harbor, I caught sight of a dear old friend—the American warship *Omaha*. I thought: If I were forty years younger, tears would spring to my eyes. The last winter I spent in Nice, this American cruiser, the *Omaha*, was stationed near by in Villefranche. At least five times a week I lunched in the sun on the beach at Villefranche, at one of those little iron tables set up in front of the hotel. For months, the *Omaha* was anchored in the harbor, a stone's throw away. It was a lovely, blue-gray ship, tidy and slim. Everyone loved its shape, its color, its big American flag, its healthy, grinning, white-toothed sailors. While we lunched, these sailors, in groups of twenty, used to row, half naked, in their giant rowboats across the blue water, in the golden sunshine of southern France. And now the *Omaha* stood here, near me, on this dark, cloudy, rainy morning—another refugee. She, too, came here from war-caught France into the not-so-blue, but at least neutral, waters. Her sailors were standing on deck, gazing at the *Rex*. The one I knew personally must surely be among them. The one who had married the pretty waitress who used to serve me my lunch, in those days when we were all still happy on the flowering French shore—the sailor, the waitress, and I.

Edith came toward me.

"American ship, isn't it?"

She couldn't understand why I was so moved.

A small steamboat brought the stranded clipper passengers from shore to the *Rex*. There were thirty or thirty-five of them. Americans, German-Jewish refugees, French non-Jews, Austrians, Hungarians, Czechs, Poles, fleeing from Paris. They came on board noisily. Our passengers surrounded them no less boisterously. Everyone spoke at once. The clipper people acted like castaways whom our great ship had rescued from the wild seas. The "old" *Rex* passengers searched feverishly among the newcomers for people they knew. Everywhere in this great, frightened, pell-mell flight—in other parts of Europe, too—every ship, every railroad train brought at least one or two people someone knew. You could be sure of it. Among those climbing up from the steamboat to the *Rex*, I immediately recognized a Viennese actor named Karin. Then, entirely unexpectedly, someone I really knew came toward me along the deck, a former colleague, Richard Horvath, who was once a cartoonist on my paper. Later he went to Berlin, where he designed women's dresses and theatrical costumes. I'd heard he was in a concentration camp. It was years since we had worked in the same office in Budapest, but now he took boarding an American-bound ship in Lisbon, and finding me on it, entirely for granted.

"Good morning," he said, without surprise.

"Thank God you're here," I said. "I understood

you were in a concentration camp. Is that true?"

"It's true."

"And—you're all right?"

"They broke one of my fingers. On my right hand. That's all."

He showed me the broken finger. It was a revolting sight. To break an artist's finger . . .

"That's nothing," he said. "Sixty-five of us were murdered."

"But I didn't see it," I said. I couldn't tear my gaze from the broken finger.

The newcomers grouped themselves around a very tall American lady, as if she were their leader. I heard later that for two whole weeks, while they waited for the ship, they did nothing but play cards in a Lisbon gambling casino. This lady, who was rich anyhow, had won the most *escudos,* and had invited them all to a big party that evening after dinner, to celebrate their "fortunate rescue." Everyone made up to her. You could see that she was used to throwing money around. Karin, the actor, in particular, never left her side. Within five minutes we had learned that this Karin, a slightly hunchbacked, aging comedian from Vienna, was a Jew. His "Aryan" wife had deserted him as soon as Austria was occupied. He had escaped. In Paris, as he told us later, he "was starving at first, and afterward fed others." He was a waiter. Made his way to Lisbon, and hung around there without a penny, until this big American woman took pity on him, and supplied him with money and an affidavit.

Horvath invited me to the party. He saw Edith beside me.

"You're not alone?"

"No."

"Oh—then bring the young lady, too."

"Thanks. May I present . . ."

That evening before dinner, Edith appeared in the corner of the bar, where we always met at that hour, in a startling, too-many-colored dress. She noticed that I looked at the dress peculiarly. She walked a few steps, swinging her hips, then turned right and left, like a model showing a gown.

"Like it?"

"Not too loud?" I asked her.

"Do you think so?"

"Yes."

She ran away. I thought she was hurt. I started after her.

"Where are you going?"

"To change my dress."

After a few minutes she came back in another dress. This one was nice, smooth, simple, just what I like. It was even a little too girlish—but I didn't want to criticize her again. I was wrong, of course. It wasn't that her dress was too young, but that I was too old for the dress. I had never thought so much about my age as since I had known her.

In the dining salon, the "castaways" all ate together at a large table. They drank before dinner, during dinner, and after dinner. In the bar, a large table was pushed together for them. They sat down, screeching and yelling, and went on drinking. Horvath, the Hungarian cartoonist, came over to get us, and we sat down at the table, too, opposite the American giantess, the dictator of the "castaways." We learned from Horvath about Emil Ormos, the Communist painter. Ormos didn't want to emigrate to America without saying good-by to his eighty-year-old mother, who lived in a village in Hungary. He left Paris with a forged passport to go home to her, but before he could see her he was arrested and sentenced to ten years in prison. The music started. We learned, too, that Geza Varadi had shot himself.

"May we dance now?" a young girl asked the beautiful tall woman.

"Of course."

"You remember Elemer Rado, the comic, at whom we used to laugh so much. He escaped to Rio de Janeiro, but his wife died on the ship," Horvath said. "Did you know that?"

"No."

Horvath introduced still another Hungarian of the "castaway" group. His name was Peter Balla. He came from Paris, too. I learned from him that a great many Hungarians had enlisted in the French army, that there was a shortage of sedatives in Budapest because no one could sleep, and also that Rudi Lorant had committed suicide.

A few people were already dancing. In Vienna, Balla said, the race law reads verbatim: "Respectable women are forbidden on pain of imprisonment to sleep with Jews." Lovers are desperate. The result is that there are women who go to the police department where professional prostitutes are registered. They apply for, and are given, prostitutes' licenses complete with photograph. Just so that they can't be considered "respectable," and can go on loving their men. And as for news of Budapest? Dr. Mor Ehrenfeld lay down right across the railroad tracks and let a train cut off his head. Edith shuddered, and said that Dr. Ehrenfeld surely couldn't have had a girl who loved him or he wouldn't have done it.

A huge wave must have hit the side of the ship, because it heeled over sharply. Glasses and plates fell down and broke with a crash. The dancing women shrieked, but neither the dancing nor the music stopped.

This same Balla mentioned the case of the young Viennese writer Alfred Erbach. Mother Aryan, father Jewish. In the light of the new laws, Erbach was a Jew and wasn't permitted to write. Erbach wanted to save his career. His mother adored him. She swore in court, under oath, that he was not the son of his father, but of her Aryan lover. So he was racially pure and was allowed to write. The story was horrible enough so far—although we'd heard plenty like it. But in Erbach's case, according to Balla, the two old people appeared together before the judge. (When he told us that, the saliva turned bitter in my mouth, as they say.) The father took the oath, too. I don't like to imagine what he swore. But he testified under oath to something from which it was obvious that Alfred Erbach could not be his son.

"He ought to be shot," Edith said.

"Who?"

"The old man's son."

"You're right," the big American woman said enthusiastically. "I like you."

The praise made Edith blush. The personal tragedies, big and small, flitted about in the loud din of the orchestra; they fluttered frighteningly in the air over the tables, like bats at evening.

"The French High Command has bromides mixed in the soldiers' red wine, in their *pinard*, as it's called."

"Why?"

"Because they want to leave the front and go home. They miss their women. And there's no fighting, anyhow. Just waiting and waiting. They're breaking down nervously from too much sexual abstinence."

"And are bromides good for that?"

"Bromides are the best cure for love."

"I've heard they always work."

"There was a big scandal about it in the Paris papers," someone said. "All the papers had articles about it."

"It was brought up in Parliament, too."

"Belgium and Holland will be blitzed, the same as Poland."

"There's a second Maginot Line on the border between France and Belgium."

"Strong?"

"Weak, they say."

The music roared out. Now almost everyone was dancing. A dapper old man, an American, came over to talk to Horvath—meantime watching Edith, who was standing beside me with her arm in mine, smiling at the old man.

"She has a magnificent figure," the old man said, turning to me.

My ear wasn't accustomed to American English yet, and I couldn't understand him in the uproar.

"Pardon me?" I said.

"I said your daughter has a magnificent figure."

I didn't correct him. Everyone went on making noise. But for the rest of the trip I avoided that man. Apparently I didn't look much younger than I was, after all. Then the hostess came over to us, too. She spoke pleasantly to me. She was a beautiful, tall woman, strong and dignified, the way I imagined the Statue of Liberty in New York Harbor. When a man led her away to dance, I looked after her with obvious pleasure.

"Do you like her?" Edith asked irritably.

"Beautiful woman."

"I didn't ask for an appraisal. Do you like her?"

"I don't like any woman especially."

"Only me."

"And not always you, either."

"Now?"

"Yes, now—unfortunately."

She was drinking. She was flushed, lively, overnoisy. Suddenly she burst out laughing.

"Why are you laughing?"

She laughed even louder.

"Am I your daughter?" she asked.

"No."

"Then what am I?"

In my feverish state, I longed for a high-sounding word, a resounding phrase.

"You are my fate," I said.

If I accidentally overheard another man whispering to a woman at a party, and heard him say a sentence like that, I would laugh or get sick to my stomach. That I could say such a thing myself shows clearly that at the time I wasn't normal. No, I hadn't been drinking—only a single glass of champagne.

Edith shrugged her shoulders. She stopped laughing. The music began a new number, an even louder one. It was a savage madness of trumpets and drums, which this little Italian orchestra conceived to be American swing.

"Want to dance?" she asked.

"No."

"Drink?"

"Yes."

We went to the bar. Two double brandies. Then two more. And at least two more, I think. The girl leaned toward me. Against the ear-splitting trumpets, she spoke right into my ear, as if it were a telephone mouthpiece.

"I'm not anyone's fate. I want to be a man's mistress or his wife or his employee. There are no other possibilities."

Everyone seemed to be drunk now. When you are drinking a lot yourself, other people seem drunker than they are. The noise was very great. Heavy waves were pounding at the ship's sides again and again. Glasses rolled, falling china tinkled, and women screamed. But they went on dancing. They shrieked and slid across the floor as if it were a lopsided skating rink. The wild, imitation swing tore at my eardrums. I remembered that I had known the Mor Ehrenfeld who had let a railroad train chop off his head. He was a surgeon.

Edith went on drinking.

"Hello." She spoke into my ear. "Edith Gaal speaking. I am not your fate."

"Oh, but you are."

"No," she shouted. She was a little tipsy. "Mistress, wife, or employee. Choose."

"*You* choose."

"I want to be all three at once."

"To me?"

"Only to you. Not to anyone else."

We were sitting on two high stools next to each other at the bar. I must have had a great deal to drink by then, because I couldn't get Dr. Mor Ehrenfeld out of my mind. Shudderingly, I imagined how he lay carefully down on the railroad embankment, so that his neck would lie exactly on one of the rails. Edith put her arm around my shoulder in an embrace. She turned to look at the dancing. She was drunk now.

"What are you looking at?" I asked.

"I'm looking at the men who are dancing. Most of them are too young for me. I don't want any of them. Only you."

I lifted her hand from my shoulder, because I saw that the old man who thought she was my daughter was looking at us as he danced.

To go to bed, I had to go down the corridor past the pharmacy, which was still brightly lighted. I stopped, hesitated a second, then went in and asked for a bromide.

"Have you a prescription?" the druggist asked.

"No, I haven't."

"Too bad. I can't give it to you without a prescription."

I went out. And so had no chance to discover the love-weakening effects of bromides. But I couldn't very well wake up the doctor in the middle of the night to ask him for a prescription for *that*. In my cabin, I sat down on my bed and closed my eyes. High above me, a train roared on its maddening way, and from the railroad embankment the head of Dr. Mor Ehrenfeld rolled down to me. The head looked at me sadly. "I don't need bromides any more," it said. I was very drunk.

CHAPTER EIGHT

THE DAY before we reached New York I was walking up and down the deck with Edith. The nearer we got to America, the more wordless these walks became, and the heavier with foreboding. I knew I was silent because my fate in relation to this girl was about to be decided. Only I couldn't tell if the emotion of parting kept me silent or if I was speechless because I didn't know how to make clear that I wanted to stay with her. I felt it was not my will which would decide the question, but some power outside myself, whose verdict I had been silently awaiting for days.

Petrovitch and Bauer came toward us. The two who had boarded the ship at Naples. Two memories of the past: Café Elysée and Café Monaco. When we spoke of them to each other, we called them "the two jolly brothelmasters."

"The last day," Bauer called gaily. "Tomorrow, New York!" He turned to Edith. "Can I speak to you alone?"

He grabbed her arm and led her a few feet away. They talked softly. Petrovitch stayed with me. The moment was an embarrassing one. Bauer laughed and slapped Edith on the behind, the way Petrovitch had when we left Naples. Petrovitch began to make conversation.

"The kid will make a lot of money in America, don't you think?"

"I've never seen her dance."

"She dances like Pavlova—plus a devil. But that's not the only way she'll make money."

I must have looked at him too hostilely.

"Don't misunderstand me," he said. "That wench has a very special talent. She doesn't go to bed with men, but she gets more money from them than the girls who do. That's why she prefers older men."

Luckily for Mr. Petrovitch, Edith and Mr. Bauer came back then. Because Mr. Petrovitch was about to get a slap in the face.

"Show it to him," Edith said to Bauer.

Mr. Bauer held a sheet of paper in his hand.

"I want her to sign this," he said.

Edith snatched the paper from his hand and gave it to me.

"Read it, please."

I glanced through the document. It was a formal contract with the night club to be opened by Messrs. Petrovitch and Bauer. It had a distinct flavor of flesh-peddling—ten per cent commission on whatever drinks guests ordered when she was with them. And a few other sickening stipulations of the same sort. I handed back the paper.

"Well?" Edith said.

"A contract," I said, my face expressing my feelings. "Should I sign?"

"No."

She turned to Bauer. "You heard him?"

"Yes."

"Well, I'm not signing."

Bauer stuck the paper into his pocket.

"Who is he, anyhow?" he asked.

"That's none of your business," Edith said.

Bauer turned to me rudely.

"Who are you?"

I told him my name and the last paper on whose staff I had worked.

"What of it?" Petrovitch said with a sarcastic smile.

Edith flew into a rage.

"He's my fiancé!"

At the word, they both gave a horselaugh. That horselaugh was my first humiliation as an exiled journalist without a job. In Budapest, Petrovitch and Bauer had been more afraid of my paper than of the police. And they were afraid enough of them.

Still neighing, Bauer asked, "What did you say? Fiancé?"

"Yes."

"A fiancé like Mr. Thomka? Or like Colonel Keery?"

I never learned the ways in which Mr. Thomka and Colonel Keery had been engaged to Edith. Edith blushed.

"Come on," she said to me.

I didn't go. I felt as if I had to hit someone. The fact that I didn't commit this stupidity was the result of my taking a moment to decide which of them I ought to hit: Petrovitch or Bauer. The Café Elysée or the Café Monaco? And in that instant it flashed through my mind that I'd already hit one person on this boat because of Edith. Another blow would have been too much.

Bauer took advantage of that moment.

"Fiancé? Divorced in two months, and unmarried up to then. We'll wait, Edith. We'll wait."

"You'll come back to Papa Petrovitch before you're through, my dear," Petrovitch said, and began to pull Bauer away by his coat.

"That'll do!" I said, shaking with rage. "That'll be quite enough of that tone!"

"Come along, Bauer," Petrovitch said. "You know I've always been opposed to giving jobs to girls who have husbands. You can just imagine how sick a bridegroom makes me!" He grinned at Edith. "You'll come back to Papa Petrovitch, crying, in torn stockings, without a cent."

"Not to me!" Bauer said furiously, and started to go.

"Never." Edith laughed. "Never. You brothel-masters. That's what you are."

Bauer turned.

"And that, my dear child, is just where you belong. You'll find that out for yourself. But then it'll be too late."

I raised my hand, but Edith threw herself in front of me. There was no fight. They went. Neighing with laughter.

"Come," Edith said, and grabbed my hand. We went back, in the opposite direction from the "jolly brothelmasters." I seemed ridiculous to myself in this role. Why was I playing Don Quixote? Up to now, Edith had lived among people like these, and nothing had happened to her. My ridiculous chivalry had probably only blocked her path to a good career.

"Thank you," she said, after we had gone about a hundred feet. "Thank you, my darling."

"Who's this Mr. Thomka?"

"A lie."

"And Colonel Keery?"

"Another lie."

"Everybody's lying?"

"Yes."

"Only not you?"

"Only not I."

We went on walking up and down. Neither of us mentioned the subject again.

Suddenly, as we were walking back and forth, an excited man ran over from the other side of the ship. His companions were standing in a group near us, and he called out to them, in a foreign language, a word I couldn't understand. They started running excitedly back with him to the other side of the boat. I thought a fire must have broken out, or someone had fallen overboard. We ran over with the others. On the opposite deck, almost all the passengers were standing close to the rail, staring at a little point of light in the distance. They didn't have to tell me what it was. I could guess. The first American light. The first gleam. Land! America. Someone was saying that in the days when ship traffic was heavy, small boats almost keeled over because of this point of light, since everybody on shipboard ran to the side from which you could see it. Our big ship didn't even waver. There were about a hundred of us crowded together in a tight group, staring at the tiny point of light. The atmosphere was tense. I think most of us would have liked to cry. The under lip of an old man standing near me was twitching. My throat was tight. If only Americans knew what America meant to us!

A voice spoke to me.

"It's moving, isn't it?"

And a hand reached for mine. Pali said the rest with his eyes. With a peculiar look, repentant but reproachful, in which there was also a tiny hint of a smile. With the tightness still in my throat, I took his hand. When he said nothing, I spoke.

"Feeling better?" I asked, uncomfortably.

"Yes," he said. "I'm all over it."

A fine-grained, snowy rain was beginning to sting our faces. While Pali and I were shaking hands, Edith suddenly hurried away, mumbling something about packing.

"Wait!" I called. "Where are you going?"

"I told you, to pack."

"But all your clothes were packed long ago."

"There are still a couple of little things left," she said as she hurried on.

I called after her again, because, frankly, I didn't want to be left alone with Pali. I was sorry now I'd let him make up with me so easily.

"You've got plenty of time, Edith, stay here."

She looked at me and laughed out loud. She was evidently laughing at my embarrassed expression, my uncertainty.

"Don't laugh," I said, annoyed. "I know you're only running away to leave me alone with Pali."

It's only now, writing this, that I realize just how childish I was at that moment. When a man is jealous, even in his fifties he may suddenly grow forty-five years younger—for a moment or two.

"Yes," she said, laughing heartily, "you're right. I just wanted to leave the two of you alone. You have something to straighten out between you. Two refugees oughtn't to be on bad terms, particularly over a good-for-nothing girl like me."

She ran off, toward the cabins. I turned and was about to call her back, but Pali took me by the arm, dragged me into the bar, and ordered a drink. He sat down on one of the high stools. I continued to stand stupidly beside him. I was still puzzled as to why I had made up with him. Under the influence of America's first light? He was speaking softly to me, but I simply couldn't listen. The first snatches of conversation which I understood clearly went something like this:

"Is it worth it . . . two decent men . . . over a little whore . . ."

That hurt. But I kept quiet. I didn't protest against the word, although I knew—I mean, I believed—that Edith was not what he called her. Partly the fear of being ridiculous kept me quiet, partly because . . . God knows . . . even if the term was a calumny, it sounded almost justified coming from Pali.

Then I heard, "We men must stick together."

I remember making some false-sounding remark in agreement, although I didn't ever again want to stick with him, of all people. Merely being with him for these few minutes had been more than enough for me already. Too embarrassing. We two couldn't possibly stick together, I thought, for the simple reason that he was a different kind of person from me. His way of thinking was normal; mine was morbid. I sighed, because this was the first time it had ever occurred to me that there was anything morbid about me. I'd never been morbid in my relations with women. I was more normal than Pali, because my interest in women was more limited than his. I had only caught this sickness in the train between Domodossola and Stresa. Like the flu.

Through the big glass door we could see more and more American lights. Out on deck, in front of the bar, people were standing in little groups, staring silently in the direction of the lights. Edith came in and ordered a drink. I didn't like what I read in her face. She was pleased that we had made up. Women aren't generally pleased with such a reconciliation unless they want to hold both men. It's normal for a female to be filled with pride when males engage in a life-and-death battle for her—and one defeats the other. I took Edith's conciliatory half smile for contempt. I deserved it. She was quite right, I deserved it.

Edith and Pali were discussing where we should stay. It turned out that no one was meeting any of us. There would be many hundreds of people on the pier, but not a single one of them would be there for us. Edith's aunt, who had sent her the affidavit, lived in Chicago.

"I'll only go to her when my last cent is gone," she told Pali. "As long as I have one red cent, I'm going to keep out of her way."

A friend of Pali's, a Hungarian photographer, lived on Long Island; but his sponsors expected him in Hollywood. Someone had told Edith about the Hotel Grindale in New York.

"It's cheap and clean, and on the West Side," she said, very decidedly.

Buxter's had been recommended to me.

"It's cheap and clean, and on the East Side," I said belligerently. We both fell silent. The names of the two cheap hotels were left hanging in the air. In my imagination, they glared at each other like two vicious dogs on the street, just before they leap at each other.

"Now that I'm approaching this huge city," Edith said, "I'm beginning to feel for the first time how alone I am."

She looked at me.

"Come to the Grindale with me."

I answered, as though no one knew more about the cheap hotels in New York than I.

"Buxter's is better. I'm not going to the Grindale."

"Please come," she said. "I don't want to be alone among seven million strangers. Aren't you at all worried about me?"

Now through the fog and the snowy rain, we saw thousands of lights. Or millions? I didn't answer. The girl looked at Pali.

"I'm only staying in New York a day," Pali said apologetically, although no one had asked anything of him. "Tomorrow noon I'm going on to my friend in Long Island, and then directly to Hollywood."

No one spoke. Then Pali turned to the girl.

"Is the Grindale a good place?"

"So they say," Edith answered.

"Very well, then. I'll go there for tonight, too," Pali said casually, but as if someone had begged him to go there.

We landed in snow, rain, and mud. I threw myself into a taxi in as matter-of-fact a way as if I were at home in Budapest. As I said good-by to Edith and Pali, I forced myself to feel that I would never see either of them again. The taxi driver was just as shabby and unshaven as taxi drivers in Budapest or Vienna. From the way he grinned at us when we said good-by in Hungarian, I was certain he understood Hungarian, as I later discovered so many of his fellow drivers did.

Pali and Edith threw their luggage into another taxi. With her hand on the handle of the taxi door, Edith turned to me.

"Won't you come with us?"

"No."

Defiantly, I gave the driver the address of Buxter's. We started. In mud and rain. The mud, the rain, the gasoline-soaked air, too mild for January, the lights, the taxi driver—at that first moment everything was just like any large city in western Europe. You have to live here a long time before you discover that the mud has a higher oil content, the air smells different, smiles mean something different, clouds come from somewhere different and go somewhere different, insects sting differently, birds are different, pneumonia is different, food, drink—everything. You learn all this slowly and at great cost. The bitterest disappointment awaits those who waltz off the ship, gay and cheerful, and, believing in appearances, feel instantly at home.

Rows of lights, rows of lights . . . only not rows of lights strung horizontally, but linked vertically to each other. That was new. Little glowing rectangles, reaching to the sky. After Paris, this street, glowing with neon lights, rain—dirty, muddy, did not seem different. It almost seemed like an imitation. But these windows lit to the sky! This striving toward something quite different from what we strive toward over there!

At Buxter's I undressed immediately and went to bed. To sleep the night through, to sleep the night through at last, after all the restless nights on shipboard. Not to have to fear what I feared night after night on the boat—that she would knock. To be alone! Beautiful thought! And I cherished the idea that to-morrow morning I would be in a different state of mind. One healthier, freer, less woman-bound. I always had a superstitious faith in some such change of mood between evening and morning. Even counted on it. For a short time (I hoped it would last at least till morning) I had the feeling I was rid of the girl. I decided, with the optimism of the convalescent, that the cause of the whole thing was only our being locked up together in the train and on the ship. But now we were living far apart, in two separate houses in the greatest sea of houses in the world. So I felt secure, and lay cozily in my comfortable bed with the sweet sense of sudden recovery. Never again. Never again. Thank you, God, that this once You pulled me back "from the edge of the abyss!" Never again!

After an hour I lit the bed-table light and got out of bed. I dressed, went downstairs, and hailed a taxi.

"Hotel Grindale on West Eighty-eighth Street."

At the desk of the Hotel Grindale, an old, be-spectacled clerk peered at me.

"Miss Gaal?" I asked.

"Who? Spell it, please."

I looked around to be sure no one could hear, I was so ashamed.

"G-a-a-l," I said in a low voice.

He looked in a large, open book.

"Room 1125."

There were a lot of names in the book. I couldn't resist it. I asked, "And—Mr. Maybaum?"

I spelled that name, too, without his asking. The clerk looked in his book. It was a strangely tense moment.

"Room 640," he answered.

I took a deep breath of relief. He wasn't living with her. Not even near her. He was living five stories below. Relieved, I went toward the elevator. The evening papers were piled high on the desk. The top paper carried the headline, "200,000 murdered in Poland." As I passed the heaps of papers on my way to the elevator, I felt the hot color rush into my face. The world was going up in flames, and I—I was taking a deep breath of relief.

CHAPTER NINE

I KNOCKED ON the door of 1125. I could hear someone come to the door and turn the key.

"Who's there?" Edith asked.

"It's I," I answered.

She opened the door. She was standing there in a pale-blue slip, short and transparent. Almost naked. I had never before found her so pretty. I was seeing her undressed for the first time, as she stood there, graceful, in a little scrap of silk. But it is typical of the degree to which I was in love with her that my delight was not so much aroused by her finely molded body. I still insist I was chiefly enchanted by her profile, which, in the light of one of those head-high American standing lamps, seemed to have a better, more sculptured outline than ever before. (It occurs to me that I may be succeeding in slowly building up a picture of myself in the course of these notes. To see a pretty dancer, with a perfect figure, naked for the first time, and to be smitten with her profile . . .)

I felt there was nothing I could say at that moment which wouldn't sound ridiculous. I threw my arms around her with savage strength. I could almost hear her bones creak. But my wise silence ended abruptly.

"Why did you open the door when you were naked?" I asked—after that embrace.

"I asked who it was, and you answered," she said.

"But when you asked, you were at the door already and had unlocked it. So when you went to the door, you must have expected someone you were going to let in. But if this person were, say, a telegraph messenger, or a waiter, or a hotel employee, you would have had to put something on before you unlocked the door."

She smiled.

"What are you getting at? That I knew you'd knock?"

"No."

"What then?"

"That you thought it was Pali."

She laughed.

"No, I knew it was you."

"How?"

"I just knew."

"Why are you lying?"

"Don't torture me. Just be glad you're here."

She leaped at me with the abandon of a happy child. Or to be more precise, the way a miserable little dog jumps at its master after it's been left at home, sad and alone in the dark, and he comes back at last, late at night. She kissed me, bit me, laughed.

"I was so sure you'd come."

"Liar," I said, almost suffocated by her kisses.

Abruptly she dropped the fierceness and gazed at me seriously out of great, wide-open eyes.

"I don't deserve to be called that," she said. "If you really want to know, Pali had already knocked at the door. An hour ago."

"And?"

"I wasn't undressed yet. I'd just begun to unpack. He invited me to go to some night club with him for a drink and dancing. I didn't go. Not because I was afraid of him. But I knew you'd come."

She sat down on the bed and made me sit down beside her. It was very warm in the room. I remembered someone in Geneva saying that in New York all the rooms are overheated. Suddenly the story of my trip from Geneva to New York tore through my brain. A few days ago I was still in Geneva. And now I was sitting in a warm room at the other side of the globe. The Poles were dying by the thousands in the snow on their frozen highways. And what would be the fate of the French, whom I loved so dearly? I felt her hot hand on my knee.

"It's good to have you here," she said. "It's good to sit beside you. Do you find it good, too?"

"Yes," I said.

(I thought of the French, for whom it wasn't good.)

"Will you stay?"

"I don't think so."

(And of the Poles, lying dead in the ditches beside the highways.)

"Then why did you come?"

"I don't know."

"I do."

"Yes? Then why did I come?"

"So as never to go away again."

No, it wasn't for this I had come to America. Not for such pleasant, sensual moments. But to spend the few years still left me, at fifty-two, at a job which might be useful to other men. I had often said that, even if I wrote and spoke until I was blue in the face, I couldn't do anything now to help mankind. But that's the fine thing about it, I thought—the fact that one must try to do something, anyhow. Even without hope. Because anyone who doesn't try is a scoundrel. I came here to redeem my last years, not to destroy them. I didn't travel across the ocean, to the other side of the world, to throw this insignificant virgin, sitting beside me, down on a bed. I didn't come here to become the slave of a hundred and twenty pounds of warm flesh, and I . . .

I gazed at her as if now, for the first time, I was finding out how her face really looked. She was still new to me, she and the whole situation, an attachment like this for a female. Never before had I been so infected by a woman. It's certainly not a nice word, but it expresses exactly what I mean. And . . . I didn't have enough money for this sort of thing . . . and when what I had was used up, and it came to my having to earn enough money for two, what could I do? You can't wash that many plates; you can't shovel that much snow; you can't deliver that many telegrams. And even if that were possible . . . I'm completely inexperienced, haven't the slightest idea how to live with a woman. My bachelor's mind couldn't even begin to imagine opening the closet and finding a pair of woman's shoes in it . . . and . . . it's hard to think this through in all its details . . . the whole thing is awful.

For some moments, I had been hearing snatches of conversation from the adjoining hotel room—1127—but I couldn't understand the words because we had been talking at the same time. Now we were quiet, and in the deep silence I could hear the neighbors again. As had happened so often during my wanderings from one hotel to another, a fragmentary bit of dialogue—the voices of two strangers, a man and a woman—came through the thin wall which separated the bed on which I was sitting from theirs. I confess I was always intrigued by such conversations, and listening to them, I felt like some fantastic thief—stealing words.

"Why are you so set against her?" a youthful female voice was saying. "What's so unusual about it? It's only natural, Harry."

"But so soon!" Harry was saying. "So frightfully soon!"

"I don't see why that should surprise you," the woman's voice went on. "She didn't do anything so extraordinary. Her husband died and she got married again. She isn't even thirty. She only did what thousands, in fact millions, of others have done."

"But so soon!" Harry said reproachfully.

Both of us were now listening to this trifling exchange. I didn't know why, but I was deeply interested in what the man on the other side of the wall was saying. I felt he was wrong, but I liked his melancholy defense of the dead husband.

"Does it really make any difference whether she gets married now or later?" the woman said.

"It does," the man said, "because theirs was a perfect marriage. As perfect as ours. And I'll tell you something. It's an awful thing for a husband who is in love with his wife to think of himself lying in the cold ground, while his wife's in a warm bed with another man . . . the way you are now, in pink silk—and smiling."

They were quiet for a while. Then the woman's voice said:

"Will you tell me who'd have benefited by her getting married a year later, let's say? Not her dead husband, would he? Certainly not she, poor thing. She'd only have given up what they call 'the right to live' for a year. Why should she? Just so you'd have a good word to say for her now? That's mighty little comfort in exchange for a year of lonely widowhood."

"But she was with that fellow Norman even at the funeral."

"It was only decent of Norman to be with her in her sorrow. It was a fine, brave thing to do."

"Brave?"

"Yes. Brave."

The man's voice lost some of its accusing tone; instead it became a little sad as he said:

"And every day after the funeral he was with the widow from morning until night. And out of sheer bravery he even slept there a couple of nights a week."

"That's not true."

"It certainly is."

"Well, even if it is, it's none of our business," the woman's voice said. "It's nobody's business."

"Are you sticking up for her?" the man said almost sadly.

"No. But you're accusing her."

"I am not."

"Yes, you are."

"I'm not."

They were quiet for some minutes. Then the woman's voice spoke softly:

"You men would all like the kind of custom they've got . . . in India, or wherever it is . . . where they burn the widow alive at her husband's funeral."

Then they fell silent.

I was gazing at the ceiling. That's how I discovered I was no longer sitting on the edge of the bed but lying on my back beside Edith—with my clothes on—she half naked still, shameless, hot, aggressive. From the way she gazed at me, from the shudder which ran through her body when her small, naked breast brushed the coarse fabric of my suit, it was obvious that she was suffering from an acute attack of love—I could feel it, and it seemed awful to me, because I knew it was just for this reason I was lost. Because she was in love. Not because I was.

She spoke very quietly—like a sister speaking to her brother—these unsisterly words:

"Marry me."

A crucial moment, I thought instantly. I must answer sensibly. Answer honestly.

"I don't ever want to get married," I said.

"To me, though. To me."

"I don't know you at all."

"Is that so important, if you love me?"

"Are you so sure I love you?"

"Absolutely sure. I'm not even asking you. I know. Am I wrong?"

"I don't think so."

"Well, then, if . . . ?"

Like a parrot, I spoke aloud what, up to then, I had been constantly repeating in my thoughts.

"I didn't come to America for that."

She bent her head over mine. Eye to eye. Mouth to mouth. To give myself courage, I said things like, "Two weeks ago I didn't know you were alive."

And I said, "Who are you, anyhow?"

From above, she looked down at me, laughing down into my face.

"I am your property. I am your flesh and your bones. Can't you tell?"

The words were much too literary. They annoyed me. She had surely read them somewhere.

"Don't you want more than this?" she asked. "Take anything. It's all yours . . . even without marriage."

"No."

I tried to sit up. She wouldn't let me. It was a ludicrous little tussle.

I said imploringly, "I don't want to see you any more. I'm running away. Perhaps it's still possible. I want to live alone."

I was determined to be brutally frank.

"I can't get on with women," I said. "I don't know how to act when I'm jealous. Whether to fight a duel or whether to conceal the humiliating pain with an embarrassed smile. I don't know how it's done—this suffering because of a woman. I've always had contempt for men who suffered because of women."

I wanted to make it even more direct, even more credible.

"I can't sleep in the same room with a woman," I said. "I can't share the same bathroom with a woman."

I had a picture of myself as being very original and admirable in my unbounded honesty. And it was nothing but a stupid, tragicomic pretense, subterfuges instead of the one great truth: I quite simply feared for my life. Not for the privacy of my bathroom. I silently prided myself that everything I said was manly, sober, and upright. Then why did everything I said hurt me so? Why did it wound me so unbearably? I have a secret superstition that anything for which there is a remedy cannot hurt unbearably. That unknown, but still existent remedy heals the pain from a distance—

like some sort of wave radiation. When anything is as painful as this, it is proof that the condition is incurable, the problem insoluble.

The girl was bending over me. She looked into my eyes, questioning, exploring. As if her flushed young face, her sparkling eyes, her bursting-ripe-tomato mouth, had hypnotized me.

"Even from this close, you don't look fifty-two," she whispered. "Or even forty-two. You look thirty-two—at most."

Suddenly, in that instant, I realized what hurt me so unbearably. It was the twenty-five or thirty years too late that I had met her. There was no remedy for that. I couldn't act like Pali Maybaum. Quickly savor an hour or day's adventure to the end—and go my way. I'm a terrible Philistine—a tragic one. It hurt me, that night, to know I would have to die much sooner than she—would have to leave her behind, young, fresh, glowing, just when I loved her most, perhaps. At best, by the time she was a beautiful, ripe, experienced woman, I would be a stealthy sigh on her lips, since she would not dare sigh aloud for the dead, in front of her new man. I would be a powerful, perhaps even victorious, rival over this new man. And everyone would know it except me.

"You are twenty," she said, as she kissed me.

"Why are you lying?"

"I'm not lying. To me you're twenty."

"To me . . . I'm a hundred, when I think of you."

"Then don't think of me."

"Tell me how not to think of you. I haven't much money, but I'd give you all I have, if you'd tell me a sure way not to do that."

I'm twenty-five years too late. I should be twenty-seven now. There was no thought which could soothe that thought. There were only chemical preparations: validol, valisan, baldrian, adalin, phenobarbitol, abasin . . . How well I know them all! Thank God for chemists. And luminal, nembutal, sedormid, phanodorm, sodium-amytal, veronal . . . nothing but peace, calm, sleep. At that time I still didn't know mankind's best friend, morphine.

My voice trembled as I snapped at her, almost angrily, "Let me out of this."

"Out of what?"

"Out of this thing. Out of all that . . ."

"You're free, you know. Go."

"No, not like that. Not with words."

"Do you want it in writing?"

"Idiot! Do something. Something mean, disagreeable. Something that would make a person go and . . ."

"If I did, you'd want to stay more than ever."

She was right. She was voicing my secret thoughts. I still insist she was stupid. But, like all women, she understood *that*. (It's typical of me, too, that even now I still maintain she was neither intelligent nor beautiful.)

"Give me some advice," I begged her. "How can I save myself from you?"

"There's only one solution."

"And that is?"

"Marry someone."

"Didn't you even hear what I was telling you before?"

"Oh, yes. But there's no other possibility. You asked for my advice. Believe me, there's no other honest advice. I gave the same advice to someone once before. He took it, and today he's a happy man, with a beautiful, chubby child. Even though he was very much in love with me."

"And you?"

"I didn't love him. I love you, though. And I'll be unhappy about you."

"Forever?"

"No. For a very long time, but not forever. I'm young. I can get over sorrow. At least, I hope so. That's our greatest strength—young people's, I mean. We know how to get over things. You ought to marry an American woman, suitable to your age. Someone quiet, serious, and decorative. A widow, let's say. You can find any number of them here. You have a nice face. You're the type women like at first glance. Get married."

Was there conceivably something else to do about it, except consider what quick-working sedative I could beg from a druggist or doctor at night now? Phanodorm? Veronal?

Through the window, thousands and thousands of other windows gleamed in the night. Didn't the light ever go out in these many millions of windows? Didn't they ever turn out the lights at night here?

It seemed to me that the girl had said something about my having temperature again. I already felt the thermometer in my mouth. This time I had a real fever, a high fever. Not from emotional or physical excitement. This time it was common influenza. But it began with a nasty high fever. I saw her running around the room, grabbing up pieces of clothing, and dressing quickly. I heard her say she was just going to run down to the drugstore for aspirin. She'd have rum sent up, too. And make tea.

At the door she called back, "Get undressed in the meantime, and into bed."

She disappeared, slamming the door with a bang. I lay for a while with my eyes closed, motionless on the bed. Now that I was alone, I began to be conscious of the great heat which was coursing through my body, and to hear the humming in my ears. I was thirsty. I got out of bed and staggered to a small desk where I saw a drinking glass. I sat down at the desk. A pile of writing paper and envelopes, with the address of the Hotel Grindale printed on them, lay in front of me. I seem to have forgotten both my thirst and the glass, because I began writing on a sheet of notepaper. As I see it now, the high fever must have set up a kind of intoxication in me. I wrote a letter to my lawyer in Budapest, in which I asked him to send my marriage and divorce papers to me in New York immediately, the originals and English translations, each document notarized by the American consulate in Budapest. But without delay. I addressed the envelope and sealed it, without having explained the reasons for my request to the lawyer. In the intoxication of the fever, it made me almost happy to think that I was going to marry a "quiet, serious, decorative woman, suitable to my age." A quiet, industrious woman, about fifty, who had some sort of business in which I could work, too. The awful part of it was that, when I closed my eyes and tried to imagine her, this serious fifty-year-old woman stood before me in a short, pale-blue slip, and on her neck she wore Edith's head.

I staggered out into the hall and, with the letter in my hand, went down in the elevator to buy stamps from the night clerk and mail the letter.

"How much?" I said, and held out the letter to him.

The clerk looked at the envelope.

"Is it urgent?" he asked.

I wouldn't have expected the first really embarrassing question to come from this stranger.

"Yes," I said, and swallowed in discomfort.

"Thirty cents, then," the clerk said, "and the letter will go to Europe by clipper. It'll be in Budapest in a week."

"Thanks."

I bought the stamp and dropped the letter into the mail box. The clerk observed my conduct with some disgust. He obviously thought I was dead drunk. I went up again, and back to the girl's room. I started to get undressed, but I only half succeeded. I grew so tired that I lay down on the bed only partly undressed, with my shoes on. I pulled the cover over me, because I was so cold by then that I was shivering. I closed my eyes so as not to have to see the many little lighted rectangles through the window. Since I had arrived in America I had seen nothing but little glowing squares in the night, reaching to the sky . . .

I must have been lying like that for several minutes when there was a knock on the door. I didn't answer. I seem not to have closed the door properly when I came in, because it opened a little now. A head appeared in the opening. I didn't recognize him immediately. It was only when he came closer to me that I saw it was Pali. He was drunk.

"Where's Edith?" he asked.

I didn't answer. He sat down in an armchair, crossed his long legs, and started to speak in a low voice, taking great care—with the age-old caution of intoxicated men—not to stutter.

"You must forgive me," he said. "I listened at the door. It was absolutely quiet in here. I thought Edith must be asleep already, and either you'd never come at all or you had left already. Know what I mean? Otherwise I would not have come. Know what I mean? The little whore told me you were certainly going to come to her tonight, but you wouldn't sleep here. She said when you left—know what I mean?—she was going to call me up. But she didn't call me up. So I came up. Why should I lie to you? I thought you didn't come. That's a fact. I'm tight, know what I mean? I thought you were here all right, but you'd gone home already."

I propped myself up on my elbows in the bed and looked him in the eye.

"Do you love her?" I asked.

"I wouldn't go quite that far," he answered. "But words fail me to describe how much such perfectly shaped legs please me."

Then he asked, "What time is it?"

Edith's wrist watch was lying on the bed table. I glanced at it.

"Half-past three," I said. I let my head fall back on the pillow and closed my eyes.

CHAPTER TEN

Exactly forty-nine and a half hours later, at five o'clock on a Thursday morning, there was—as they say in the biographies—a turning point in my life. I had my first heart attack.

By then, I had been lying in Edith's bed for two whole days. I had been lying there since that Tuesday morning when she went down for the aspirin, and told me to undress and lie down, because I had a high fever. Pali had gone before Edith came back with the aspirin. They must have met in the hall, because when Edith came in she casually let drop:

"I thought I saw Pali in the hall—going away from here—toward the other elevator."

She looked at me questioningly. I didn't answer. Either she took this silence for an answer or attributed it to the fever. Perhaps I was mistaken, but, at the time, I felt that she was grateful for my silence. She forced aspirin into me, and gave me hot tea, into which she poured enormous quantities of rum. My forehead and cheeks were burning with fever. I was drunk from the rum, and from what Pali had said. Later, toward morning, Edith disappeared again, but she soon reappeared beside my bed with a Dr. Knopfler. Just where she got this doctor I had no idea. Up to then I had never heard of this refugee doctor, who had escaped from Vienna. Later it turned out that she had had his address in her little notebook. A friend had recommended him to her. It still makes me smile to think of Dr. Knopfler, tall, thin, pale, with his Christ-like face and Christ-like beard. As I afterward learned, the friend didn't recommend him to Edith as a doctor. On the contrary, when she gave her his address, she added the information that Dr. Knopfler was "a confirmed spiritualist but liked pretty girls."

Because of the high fever, Edith refused to let me get up. She wouldn't let me go back to the Buxter. I must stay here, here in her bed. She rented a small box-like room, opposite mine on the same hallway, and moved there. She went to the Buxter, got my things, and paid for the full day which they charged for the few hours I had spent there. All day Tuesday she worked, rushed about, got out of breath, spent money, telephoned, ran to the drugstore, boiled water, and got upset. I was burning with fever. I saw Dr. Knopfler's tall, haggard shape twice a day, both Tuesday and Wednesday. In my stupor, it seemed to me I overheard them whisper the word "pneumonia." But I had a feeling he was putting Edith's mind at rest about pneumonia. It annoyed me that Edith hadn't cashed the check I gave her. For days the check lay on the little desk where I had written the letter to my lawyer that first night, asking him to send me my divorce papers. She spent her own money for the rum, the medicines, everything that was needed. From one day to the next this unknown traveling companion, who two weeks before I hadn't known was alive, had become my mother, my wife, my child. (Unfortunately, considering the difference in our ages, chiefly my child.) She had become the only support I had in the world. To me, America was even stranger and bigger than it was to other newcomers, because I didn't know a soul here. I came blindly, like a person who runs from something in the night and does not know where he is running. Hungarians in America? They say there are about 100,000 in New York alone. Even so, I felt alone. It was possible that some of the émigré journalists I knew had arrived here before me. But so far I hadn't looked for them and didn't even know their addresses. I was defiant, proud, and lonely. I wouldn't beg for money or for social relationships, either. Besides, I had landed on Monday evening, and unfortunately by Tuesday morning Dr. Knopfler, looking troubled, was already taking my temperature.

I hadn't seen Pali again. I had heard that, the same morning, after that nasty scene, he had left the Hotel Grindale and gone to Long Island to stay with his friend, the photographer. Pali, I had decided by then, was an immoral rake, a liar. Edith swore that, although she had spoken to him that night, she had not asked him to come to her room. So Pali had been lying. Or Edith. Or both. Let's drop it.

Early Thursday morning, then, the great event oc-

curred. At five o'clock I was torn from a deep sleep by
a violent fit of coughing. This had barely ended, at
long last, when I began to notice that I could only
breathe with great difficulty. I couldn't seem to get any
air into my lungs. For a while, I thought it was only a
passing discomfort. But the condition began to grow
more and more agonizing, until I was really frightened.
I had hardly enough strength to pick up the telephone
receiver and call Edith's room. Edith was terrified, and
came running over to my room with nothing on but
her fur coat over her nightgown. By now I was thoroughly alarmed, too, because I believed my end was
near. Edith telephoned excitedly; but she spoke softly
into the mouthpiece so that I couldn't hear what she
was saying. I gasped clumsily for breath, like a fish out
of water. Later, when I was utterly miserable, an
elderly man with a black bag in his hand came into the
room. He was the hotel doctor. He threw open the
window. He gave Edith orders. They wrapped me in
a blanket and carried me out of the bed to the open
window. There they put me down, and the doctor
turned my face so that the cold January air could flow
over it. Then he hurried into the bathroom. I heard
him say he had to sterilize his needle for an injection.
Then he came back into the room, and stuck the needle
in my thigh. With the simple naïveté of a sick man, I
tried to determine whether the doctor was frightened
or not, in order to figure out whether my condition
was dangerous. He wasn't. Later I realized why he

wasn't frightened. Because it wasn't he, but I, who was having the heart attack.

I watched myself from minute to minute, but my condition didn't improve. The doctor said something about having patience; I shouldn't worry; I'd be better soon. Gasping for breath, I asked him if he'd handled cases like this before. "Oh, plenty," he answered. We were waiting and watching, and I was panting quite prettily, nearly suffocating, when the tall Dr. Knopfler with the Christ-like head appeared. Edith had telephoned him at the start—this doctor about whom we knew that he was a confirmed spiritualist but liked pretty girls. As he came in the door he seemed to me twice as tall as before. I remember that when he appeared, I was breathing with somewhat more effort than before. After a whispered conference with the hotel doctor, Dr. Knopfler also went into the bathroom, sterilized a needle, and gave me an injection in the thigh, too. Simple naïveté, number two—even though my breathing hadn't improved, I got a certain sense of security from the realization that two doctors were working over me. If one made a mistake, the other would be sure to point it out to him. A moment later, when Dr. Knopfler laid his head on my exposed chest to listen to my heart, and his beard brushed against my skin, I was again overcome by fear and dismay. It was Dr. Knopfler's beard that aroused the fear. I had seen the beard before, of course, but it was only now that it took on a sinister meaning for me. I admit

I'd always been afraid of bearded doctors, just like a child. Close to suffocating, I thought: Dr. Knopfler grew that beard because it was the tradition among old-fashioned Viennese doctors to wear beards, gold-rimmed eyeglasses, and top hats. There was a popular belief that the longer the beard, the more competent the doctor. The two doctors whispered to each other. Then they went to the telephone, and the hotel doctor telephoned to someone. I was breathing a little more easily by then. I called out, still panting, that I wouldn't let them take me to the hospital. I had just as great a fear of hospitals as of doctors' beards—typical of people who've never been seriously ill and consider hospitals death factories.

"No, no. They're just telephoning for an oxygen tent," Edith quieted my fears.

"I guess it's all over with me," I gasped.

Up to then, I'd only heard about oxygen tents, but to my mind they were a last desperate attempt, something which never worked, but which the doctor felt a moral obligation to prescribe for a dying man, like, say, an injection of camphor. So it came as a most unpleasant surprise when Edith tried to console me with the words "oxygen tent," of all things.

"I guess it's all over with me," I said very softly to myself.

When the tent arrived, Edith was just making coffee for the doctors. This helped to lift my tragic mood. Besides, the heavy breathing had considerably subsided by then. When Dr. Knopfler asked me how I felt, I yawned wearily, and said, "I'm very sleepy."

"That's the morphine," Dr. Knopfler said triumphantly, as if he had discovered morphine, and put me under the tent, which was set up over the bed. It was made entirely of isinglass windows. Two men in overalls were working skillfully on the tent. I noticed them first when I was already underneath it. Then the two doctors, the two workmen, and Edith, all put their heads together. Through the tent I could hear them whispering about money. Obviously, the tent had to be paid for in advance, because people generally died under it. The men in workclothes got their money and went.

I looked around the tent. How many people had already died in this one? I was shocked by the thought. I hadn't been conscious of it before, but now I realized that I was afraid to die. This tent is a bridge to the coffin, I thought. Once in Poland in 1916, when I was a war correspondent, I found myself in a field with some Hungarian officers in the line of Russian rifle fire. There was no cover of any kind on the flat meadow. First we had to crawl on our stomachs. Then we had to run quite a stretch to a near-by woods where our artillery was stationed. We crawled through the high wheat. That was the first time I discovered that bullets really do whistle loudly through the air. Shrapnel fell, too. I only mention it because that was the first time I ran a kind of race with death. I was running

toward the woods with the others, but I felt no fear of
death. To be precise, perhaps I should put it this way:
we were afraid of the bullets, but not of death. I probably wouldn't be afraid on a battlefield now, either.
The fact that you deliberately go where there is danger
takes away much, if not all, of the fear of death. But
the idea of dying in a hospital atmosphere depressed
me. The routine of dying was a frightful thought—
the doctors, the nurses, all the white uniforms . . .
the smell of ether, the injections, the oxygen tents
. . . all the red tape of death. To die suddenly as the
result of having taken a chance, to march into battle, or
go up in a plane—that was less painful to imagine than
being snuffed out by an illness, like being executed for
a crime you didn't commit. There's an enormous difference between these two kinds of fear. I know that
now, because I've lived through both.

Edith sat in an armchair, where she could see
through the isinglass into the tent. Terribly drowsy
from the morphine, I could see her face through the
tent. She looked frightened. Dr. Knopfler stood beside
her and consoled her, patting her face frequently. I
was very drowsy. I could hardly keep my eyes open.
Automatically, the thought came to me, "Dr. Knopfler
is a convinced spiritualist, but he likes pretty girls."
In this half-waking state, I began to feel positively
well. Could it have been the effect of the morphine?
In my half sleep, I thought, "Dr. Knopfler is quite
right . . . to like pretty girls. Perhaps he's not so
right . . . about being a spiritualist . . . even though

the eternal, never-to-be-fulfilled desire of men to have some link with the dead . . . is seductively beautiful. But . . . about liking pretty girls . . . he's . . . absolutely . . . right . . ."

It was late afternoon when I awoke. It was already dark. Edith was sitting in the armchair again. Or still sitting there.

Of the following days, I have only cloudy, indistinct memories. Sometimes I slept during the day, sometimes at night. I don't quite remember eating anything but digitalis and sleeping medicine. But every time I opened my eyes and looked around me, Edith was sitting in the same spot in the same armchair. Sometimes I woke during the night, sometimes during the day. I don't know when she slept, if she slept at all. Strange . . . this strong, buoyant girl with the red hair had started out from the middle of Europe, alone, to come here to the land of promise, to make a success of her lovely long legs, dancing in a spotlight to screeching music, to turn somersaults in front of a Hollywood movie camera, to make hundreds of thousands of dollars, to live in a palace, and play a role in the exciting world of the gossip columns . . . and now she was sitting in this cheap, not too pleasant-smelling, little hotel room, beside the bed of a sick stranger—let's come right out with it—beside the bed of a sick old man, wasting the precious, never-to-be-recovered days and weeks of her youth . . . why? It's clear, I thought, she's doing it out of light-minded stupidity, out of stupidity, stupidity, stupidity. . . .

But perhaps my state of mind was the result of my feeling genuinely seasick from the injections they were constantly pushing into the veins of my arms.

One evening, after Dr. Knopfler had stuck me in the arm again, I asked a question.

"Doctor, please tell me what caused this attack? How do you get a thing like this?"

He looked at me with a queer, bitter smile.

"This being hunted . . . through all Europe . . . this flight . . . and these two years . . . the second half of '39 . . . and the little of '40 we've lived through . . . would be enough cause. Besides . . ."

He looked at Edith, then at me. Then at Edith again.

"How old are you?" he asked me.

"Fifty-two."

His glance rested on me again, but now he looked at me as if to say, "Isn't it perfectly obvious what's happened to you, my dear suicide?"

My American project? My great conception of a tremendous agency to enlighten Europe by political articles! Where was it all? The fate of the world? France's fears of death—France which had retired behind its Maginot Line—and the feeling of security, already wavering, which she had placed in that line! I'll admit that my own fear of death concerned me more. Does everyone lose his concern for the tragedy of the world as soon as his own begins? Or am I just unusually egotistical, mean, cynical?

It had all been so unexpected—that's why it affected me so powerfully. I'd thought often, before now, about how long I'd live. Do other aging men do that, too? Or is it just I who am such a coward? I remember once in Venice how I tossed in my bed through a sleepless night, thinking about it, then turned on the light, took a paper and pencil, and figured out the average lifetime of my parents, grandparents, uncles, and aunts. It came out to seventy. No wonder that at fifty-two I looked on my approaching death as a frightful and unhappy accident. Only an *unjust* death sentence by a court could have such an embittering effect on the innocent man who is condemned.

I woke again—I don't know if it was from an afternoon or nighttime sleep—and again Dr. Knopfler was sitting beside Edith, who was listening to him with a weary, bored expression on her face. I would have taken to my heels long before that if any woman had listened to what I was saying with such an expression. Dr. Knopfler always stayed longer than was necessary, because of Edith. Edith said that the poor man had plenty of time. Things were going badly for him. He had hardly any patients, and those he had were poor Austrian refugees who couldn't pay him. He spoke softly in a rather fine baritone. I liked his voice. He was always talking about Vienna. Of all the refugees in New York, the Viennese are the most homesick. I wasn't particularly fond of Vienna, but it was a point about which you couldn't argue. Strange—Dr. Knopfler really had a Christ-like face, not only because of his beard and his dreamy theosophist's eyes, but because of the look of pain in his face. Too often, at least once a day, he mentioned Professor Wenckebach. I knew this Wenckebach. He was of Dutch descent, a professor at the University of Vienna. As a heart specialist he was a genius, and acknowledged to be a sort of demi-god, even by the imperial family. I had to interview him once, when he came to Budapest by plane to see a cabinet minister who was critically ill. He really was a genius. Was he still alive? Dr. Knopfler was explaining something to Edith softly, and with a sad smile; I couldn't hear what it was from inside the tent. Poor Edith, listening so patiently to that boring man, for my sake. I was thankful to her for *this* sacrifice, too. If I had a million dollars, I thought, I'd have this Wenckebach brought from Vienna in an airplane right away, through war and through battlefields, over ocean and clouds . . . right away. I closed my eyes. In a half sleep I had a kind of fantasy—Wenckebach came, walked into the room, examined me, and said, "Your doctor is an ass. There's nothing wrong with you, take a laxative. That's all you need."

The last time I saw Professor Wenckebach, he was seventy years old. A thin, dapper man, with blond hair. He was usually only called in for consultation when it was too late, because he was so expensive. The sound of Dr. Knopfler's quiet, warm baritone, extravagantly praising him, penetrated through my tent. I sighed. How fine it would be, if it were only the other way round—if Wenckebach were sitting here extravagantly praising Dr. Knopfler.

"Look, he's smiling," Edith said, pointing to me.

Dr. Knopfler walked over to the tent, opened the little window, and spoke into it.

"Feeling better?"

"Much better," I said.

"Did my mentioning Wenckebach's name make you better?"

"Yes. That's what did it."

Afterward I was sorry I had hurt his professional pride with an answer like that. But by that time he had gone.

CHAPTER ELEVEN

LATER WHEN I was allowed to stay out of bed for about six hours a day, Dr. Knopfler asked us to sit down at the table one evening after dinner. He said he wanted to tell me exactly what regime I would have to follow in future.

"Because you must understand," he said, "that from now on you will have to lead a totally different kind of life, adapted to your illness, if you . . ."

He didn't finish the sentence, but it wasn't necessary. It was obvious that the sentence ended, "If you want to go on living." He explained this new regime intelligently in all its details. The three of us sat around the table, and Edith and I wrote down everything he said. We marked down the hours, the minutes, the foods, the drinks, the length of the walks, the amount of stair climbing, the temperature of the bath, the number of hours sleep at night and in the afternoon.

Just when I thought that everything of importance had been discussed and noted down, Dr. Knopfler commenced to tap nervously on the table with his long, skinny fingers.

After a short pause, he said to me, "And now, I'd like to have a few words with you in private."

He looked at Edith. There was another pause. What you might call an awkward pause. Edith was the first to break it.

"Do you want to talk to him about me?"

The doctor answered hypocritically.

"I want to talk to him about himself."

Edith was becoming uneasy.

"About me?"

"About his health," the doctor said. "About his relations with women."

"He has only one relation with a woman," Edith said calmly, "and that's with me. And since I can guess what you're going to say, let's come to the point right away. We don't have the kind of relation you're thinking about and never have had."

"That's none of my business," Dr. Knopfler said, but I could see that he was tormented, because he simply didn't believe what Edith was saying. The medieval martyr's face, elongated and gaunt, had become grotesque. Now Dr. Knopfler looked like a fake El Greco.

"As a doctor, I am only concerned with my patient," he said. "I don't care about his partner at all."

"And the point is?" I said impatiently.

"The point is . . . I'd like to talk to you privately."

Edith spoke sharply. "I won't leave. I tell you we have no sexual relation. And as his nurse and friend, I have a right, I even have an obligation, to hear all your orders."

A wicked little light flickered in the El Greco martyr eyes.

"As far as I'm concerned," he said, "you can stay and hear it all."

"And the point is?" I said, growing more and more impatient.

Dr. Knopfler turned to me. "I don't care with whom you've had affairs or with whom you're having one now. As your doctor, the only important thing to me is that, in future . . . for a long time to come . . . you're not to have relations with anyone. And by relations, I don't mean simply the usual sexual relations, but something which can be far more harmful from a medical standpoint, perhaps even fatal. I mean a patient's living in close contact with a woman who arouses his desires, who excites him, who is capable of tormenting him without meaning to."

"And the point is?" I said, almost rudely now.

"And the point is," he said churlishly, and with an unmistakably diabolical gleam in his martyr's eyes, "that in future you must live like an old man. Live as though you were seventy instead of fifty-two. Give up what's even commoner here in America than among us Europeans—men living as though they were at least ten years younger than they are. That's why it's not at all surprising when one of these pink-cheeked, youthful-old men walks cheerfully into a cocktail party, rushes up to the hostess, shakes her hand, looks at her with a happy smile, and falls down dead. Or an equally youthful-old man, a Senator this time, makes a speech at a meeting, ends his speech vigorously and spiritedly, then drops dead. It's my duty to make my patients realize that there are certain things for which they will have to pay with their lives. One of them is a great love like this, and living together like this, even without sexual intercourse, perhaps even more without it."

"I see," I said, and stared straight ahead of me at the notes I had made. I added, not too politely, "I noticed the other day, when you asked about my age, that you place extraordinary weight on such things."

"I repeat," he said, "there are certain things for which you might pay with your life."

Edith stood up.

"Let's leave it at that," she said. "No one could make what you wanted to say any clearer than you have. And no one could understand it any better than your patient."

"She's right," I said.

There was another painful pause.

"I'm sorry, but I must get on to another patient," Dr. Knopfler lied, and stood up. Edith gave him a warm, friendly smile. That's another one of those things I was, and still am, incapable of understanding. That warm, encouraging, almost coquettish smile offered to such a distasteful fellow after a scene like that—for no reason at all—just for the sake of smiling. I should have begun to study women forty years sooner; then perhaps I wouldn't have been so surprised at that sort of thing. Now it was too late. All I could do now was to be amazed.

After Dr. Knopfler had gone, I began to walk nervously up and down the room. What he said had touched me to the quick. If Edith had only kept quiet, what happened then would not have happened—or, perhaps, it would have happened, but long after.

"Sit down and listen to me," she said. "We must talk very seriously."

I sat down beside her. She took my hand.

"We must give each other up," she said. She tried to say it simply, but one corner of her mouth twitched with pain when she said it. You could tell she was keeping a hold on herself. She was crying with her whole body, her whole face, only not with her eyes. What made the situation so uncomfortable for me was that I was thinking the same thing—but because it was she who spoke, and not I, the words hurt me more than if I had said them.

"Does that hurt you?" she asked.

I said, because I was trying not to be sentimental, "To invent an impossible situation . . . it's exactly like . . . let's say . . . let's suppose . . . you've had dinner at someone's house . . . and it's late, and you want to go home . . . and you go up to your hostess, intending to say, 'It's getting late, I really ought to go now,' and you walk toward her, but before you can open your mouth, the lady says, 'It's getting late. You really ought to go home now.' "

"I see," she said.

It was clear to me that, if I weren't determined to the point of brutality now, I would be lost.

"You're right. We must break off," I said. "Completely and forever, as though we'd never met."

"Otherwise there'd be no sense in it," she said. "I'm not worth a fine, decent man's being destroyed for my sake."

She looked at me in a way which, for an instant, made nothing seem worth wanting but to take her in my arms and be destroyed for her, right here on the spot. But that only lasted a second. The words of the doctor with the martyr's face went through my mind like the twinge of a toothache—"You may have to pay with your life." And I remembered the look with which the doctor "devoured" Edith, just like the Finnish consul that time on the train . . . just like Pali on the boat . . . and, I haven't mentioned it before, but—let's be frank—the elderly hotel doctor whose eyes nearly popped out that Thursday when I was almost suffocating, and Edith was so frightened that she thoughtlessly threw off her fur coat, and stood in her nightgown, trying to help us. No, I mustn't stay anywhere near her, if I didn't want to be ruined. I couldn't endure the prospect of living with her, now that I knew what my disease was, now that I realized I could get along, after a fashion, with a wounded heart patched up in the nick of time, but only if I guarded it like the apple of my eye. This girl meant more to me already than a wife or child, but for that very reason I could only see her now as my potential murderer. If I didn't look at the papers, if I turned off my radio, and took three pills of phenobarbitol, there wouldn't be any world war for my sick heart. But at what shouldn't I look, what should I turn off, what should I take, if she was living in the same room with me? No, no, no. I don't want to die. And I don't want to watch tensely to see whom she smiles at, and why. I'm a born bachelor. I have to live alone. I must be strong now. I mustn't die because of a stranger, a little nobody, whom I saw for the first time a couple of days ago.

And now something else happened, a little accidental thing, but crucial. I repeat what I said before, when Edith began to speak. If it hadn't happened here and now, it would have happened the next day, or the day after that, or in a week, or somewhere else, perhaps; but it would certainly have happened.

The telephone rang. I picked up the receiver

"Hello," a voice said. "Apartment 1125?"

It was Pali's voice.

"Yes," I said. For a second there was silence on the wire, as though the connection had been broken. Pali hadn't expected me to answer.

"Pali?" I said.

"Yes," he said, embarrassed. "I wanted to say good-by to Edith. I'm leaving for Hollywood any day now."

"Are you calling from Long Island?"

"No. I'm in New York."

"Near by?"

"Yes."

"Then come over."

A short pause.

"Right now?"

"Yes. Right now."

"O. K.," he said, and hung up.

Edith was looking at me, her forehead puckered.

"What does this mean?" she asked me. I could tell that she had already guessed what it meant, and what was going to happen.

"You asked him to come here?" she said.

"Yes."

She stood up, went to the window, and looked for a long time at the street and the lighted houses across the way. A very long time. We each knew what the other was thinking. This long silence was like talking long and frankly to each other. I undressed and lay down on my bed because, according to the doctor's orders, the time had come to lie down. From the bed I looked out at the lighted windows, too. Today I know that these silent moments were our farewell. As we stared at the windows across the way, one of those platitudes you hear so often came to my mind—"Life separated them . . . " It's different with us, I thought. It's death which separates us.

Pali came then.

"Are you still sick?" he asked, when he saw that I was in bed already.

He looked from one of us to the other. He sensed that something unusual was going on. They took two chairs and sat down beside my bed, next to each other.

"Pali," I said, forcing myself to be quiet and simple,

"Edith would be willing to go to Hollywood with you if you'd like to take her."

"Oh, my God," Edith said softly. She groped for her handkerchief, and began to cry quietly. I felt that the words "Oh, my God," although they sounded despairing, carried no trace of protest. That gave me strength. It was bitter, but it gave me strength.

Pali looked at the girl in amazement.

"Did you have a fight?" he asked.

"No," I said. "We're the best of friends, and we're going to stay that way. But we can't live together. I know the reason, and so does Edith. And Edith's future is in Hollywood . . . the same as yours. You must follow your careers together."

I couldn't help it. The words were noble, fine-sounding, unselfish words, but they had a false ring, because concealed behind them was the greatest selfishness of all—the will to live.

Edith didn't say anything more; she only cried softly. I waited to hear what Pali would say, but he remained silent, too. He was staring thoughtfully in front of him, at the floor. This showed he was taking the affair more seriously than one would have expected of him. But after a minute he was his old self again.

"Are you giving her to me?" he asked with a smile, and put his arm around her. Edith brushed his arm away, got up from the chair, and sat down on the edge of the bed, next to me.

"Edith," I said to her softly, "there's no better solution."

"There is," she said, "but if you think—— Thy will be done!"

At that instant I was convinced that what she believed to be love was beginning to be overcome by her health, her youth, her natural young horror at living with a sick man, and by the longing for success which the screen writer had aroused in her. All natural, understandable things.

Pali was taking the affair very seriously, after all. With a troubled face, he began to pace up and down the room. Apparently he saw something more in Edith than just her perfect legs. The girl was silent. She wasn't crying any more. She held my hand and lowered her head so as not to have to look at either me or Pali. I felt that I had found the way to free myself of Edith, and the fact began to hurt me unspeakably. Pali stopped walking up and down, and stood before my bed, as if to announce that he had arrived at a decision. As he looked at me, I noticed that one of his eyes was twitching slightly, with a barely noticeable nervous tic. It wasn't hard to read his love for the girl in his face. He had given her up because he saw that we were in love, and now I had freed him. You could see how greatly these few minutes had upset him. I thought he would ask me questions, try to learn the reason for my sudden decision. But he said nothing. I began to speak again.

"Let's get it over with. End it. For God's sake, go. No good-bys."

I was so drenched in a kind of pain unknown to me

until then that I was afraid we would have to call the doctor again.

"Go," I said.

Pali picked up his hat from the table. The girl didn't move.

"And don't write," I said. "Send me a telegram when you get there, if you don't mind. But nothing more. Ever."

Questions and answers appeared in my brain, flew swiftly across it, and vanished, like stage clouds flashed on a backdrop to signify a storm. Ought I be ashamed of what I had done? No! I want to live. How long? I don't know. But to live on and on! Above all not to know when the hour of death is coming—let me say it without fear—the hour of suffocation. I want uncertainty! I want a reprieve! Or am I afraid to admit that I want to achieve the family average of seventy, and so am cruel to myself and to another human being? And ought I consider it a command of my conscience that, whether I wanted to or not, I was now forced to think of the many thousands of young soldiers already buried under the soil of Europe? Why weren't they as fearful for their lives as I? Am I abnormally cowardly, a monster, or am I normal and the many millions of young soldiers abnormal? Yes . . . these last months . . . the end of 1939 and the beginning of 1940 . . . these months have made me what I am. People have to live through things like that when they are young, to be able to bear them. My spiritual balance must have been disturbed by the fact that I constantly feel that nowadays private unhappiness is unjustified. I seem to myself like a thief, when I sigh for my own sorrows. I feel I am stealing that sigh from the many billions of sighs owed to mankind for all that is happening to them now.

I flinched, as Edith spoke.

"Pali, go now."

"You too," I said to Edith.

"No," she said, "I'm staying here, just as I always do, until the night nurse comes at nine."

"I'm staying at the Hotel Sunfield," Pali said. "S-u-n-f-i-e-l-d. It's in the phone book."

"All right," Edith said. "I'll come in the morning . . . to talk about the trip. I'll spend tonight in my room here."

She made me a present of that, that Pali-less night. Pali went out.

When we were alone, I said, "Let's promise each other not to discuss it, not to explain, not to say another word about the whole matter."

She stood up and turned to me. "Mayn't I even say that I only love *you*."

"No," I said.

"Mayn't I even say that I can understand your sending me away?"

"No," I said.

"Or even that I swear to God I'm only going because of what the doctor said?"

When I didn't answer, she added, very low, "That I'm only going to save your life?"

Her voice had a ring of sincerity. But it wasn't the ring of sincerity that made me believe what she said, but the way she had acted in the past days. Even so, I said in the sarcastic tone of a disagreeable invalid:

"Why did you stay? Even though I begged you to go with Pali. I begged you to get it over with . . ."

She pressed her lips together to show she was deliberately keeping still.

"Go," I said. "Go, my darling."

She didn't budge.

"Why don't you go?"

She knelt beside the bed and laid her head next to mine on the pillow. She spoke in a whisper.

"Tomorrow Pali will have me. If not tomorrow, then later. But I want to give myself to you. What else have I to give you? Then I promise you, you'll never see me again."

She was crying bitterly, with a great many tears, and no handkerchief. She burrowed her head in the pillow like a child crying in bed—in bed, where they cry best. Nowhere else so well, nowhere else so bitterly.

"Let's sleep with each other today, for the first and last time. So you can be the first . . . so I'll belong to you . . . the first time. Then, so help me God, you'll never see me again."

I didn't answer. I was pressing my lips together now.

"Answer me," she said. "It's almost nine. The nurse will be here any minute. If you want me, I'll send the nurse away on some pretext and tell her that I'll take her place tonight."

She waited a long time for my answer.

"No," I said softly, and felt that I was hateful.

We were silent again, motionless, for a long time. Now, writing it down, I'd like to leave twenty or thirty sheets of clean white paper empty—that's how I could best explain how long we were silent. Then there was a knock on the door. Edith got up and let the night nurse in. The night nurse was a woman of gigantic build, very masculine in appearance. She smiled at me from behind her glasses, asked how I was, and disappeared into the bathroom to put on her white uniform. Edith bent over me. She whispered almost inaudibly in my ear.

"Yes?"

I whispered the answer.

"No."

The nurse came out of the bathroom in a snow-white, starched uniform, gave me the small thermometer, and took my pulse. That was the first thing she did every evening. While I was taking my temperature, Edith opened the box that held the white capsules of sleeping medicine. It was standing on the little bed table. I took one of these capsules regularly at ten o'clock, but it was only nine now. We usually opened the capsules and shook the white powder out onto a spoonful of water. I took it that way, because it worked faster. This time Edith opened two capsules and shook their contents into the spoon.

"What are you doing?" I asked, giving the thermometer back to the nurse. She read the thermometer and wrote a number on a piece of paper.

Edith smiled.

"To judge by how painful all this is to me, it must be very painful to you, too," she said.

She handed me the spoon with its double dose.

"Sleep," she said.

The nurse peered at the spoon.

"Isn't that too much?" she asked.

"No," Edith said. "The doctor ordered it for today."

The nurse looked at her watch.

"But it's still too early for him to take it. It's only a few minutes after nine."

"I want him to get to sleep as early as possible today and have a long sleep—the doctor does, too," Edith said.

She held the spoon to my mouth. I swallowed the white powder. She was putting me to sleep, like a doctor, so the operation wouldn't hurt. She stood silently beside the bed, a long, long time. Until I fell asleep. And her picture remained like that in my memory— glowing red bush of hair under the light of the lamp, a kindly, almost motherly, smile, and behind and above her the huge nurse's strong, spectacled, mannish face.

CHAPTER TWELVE

Six weeks later, I was married. I married Mrs. Hilda Cole, a forty-eight-year-old widow, quiet and pleasant-looking. I still can't believe that it's true. And I still wish it were only a dream. But it isn't a dream. I'll explain how it happened.

At the end of February, the weather grew unusually springlike. I'd heard a good deal about the whimsicality of New York weather, but even so, I was startled by the mild, sunny mornings, reminiscent of the French Riviera, which shone suddenly out of a cruel winter. On one of these lovely days Dr. Knopfler, to whom I went from time to time for a checkup, asked me, "By the way, what do you do all day long?"

"Make plans. I've been down to the *New York Times* and the Public Library already. I'm going to start working soon."

"Don't begin to work yet," he said. "Hurry and get some use out of this fine weather. Go away somewhere for a couple of weeks. Rest. Get yourself in condition. You've been in bed a long time, and gone through a lot. You're a little anemic, too. Good air, a beach, slow strolls."

"Yes . . . yes . . ." I said thoughtfully, while he

wrote down the names of four or five places on Long Island. Then, as he always did at least once during every visit, he brought the conversation around to Edith again.

"Does it make you nervous, not having Edith any more?"

"Not especially."

"Do you miss her?"

"Why should I miss her? I only knew her for a few weeks."

"Sometimes we only know people a day, and still miss them when they go."

"People are different," I said, hoping the generalization would stifle his somewhat officious interest. I could tell that he missed her. Though he hadn't known her even as long as I had. I had a distinct feeling that he blamed me for letting Edith disappear from the little circle where he might have met her.

"Take a trip," he said, while I was standing, naked, in front of the X-ray machine.

"Do you see anything in my insides that makes a trip imperative?"

"No. Lie down here."

He stretched me out, pounded me, listened to my heart, had me do exercises, and took my blood pressure.

"Pretty good," he said, reassuringly. And added what had become the refrain of these examinations:

"Just as long as you live carefully, the way you're doing, you'll . . ."

"I'll go on living?"

"You'll have done everything possible to go on living."

"A cautious formulation," I said bitterly.

"Prophecy is a risky business," he said, and took me to the door. His El Greco martyr's face, with its skimpy beard, was gaunter and paler than ever. Maybe he needs a doctor, too, I thought.

There was no news from Hollywood after the telegram saying they had arrived, and giving Pali's address, a second-rate studio. No world-shaking news came from the east, either. The European disaster seemed to have reached a deadlock. The French, following some incomprehensible plan, were moving forward by inches across the Maginot Line, into German territory. As a newspaper reader, I was a great, though distant, admirer of Gamelin. In Switzerland, I used to say to everyone, "I don't understand a thing about it, but Gamelin undoubtedly knows what he's doing." And Sumner Welles went to Europe, and visited one capital after another to confer with the rulers of the world. The cashier of the Hotel Buxter, who was my only real American friend, said that that could only mean one of two things—world peace or America's entry into the war. I'd been at Buxter's again for five weeks now. I'd moved back to be rid even of the memory of the Grindale. I wrote to the hotels the doctor had recommended, for their prices. After careful figuring, I had decided to follow his advice and spend a few weeks in some quiet spot, recuperating.

A few days before I left, I met Richard Horvath, the

costume designer, on the street. The one who had boarded the ship in Lisbon with the clipper castaways —the Hungarian designer with the broken finger. I would never have believed you could accidentally meet anyone on a New York street. The towns where I lived in Europe weren't exactly small, but we always imagined New York as so big, and with so terribly many streets, that you'd never meet anyone you knew. If you stand on the main thoroughfare of a small town, you'll notice that people are constantly greeting each other. In Paris, it's fairly unusual to see people greet each other on the street. I once sat for hours on the Champs-Elysées on a Sunday in spring. Thousands of people strolled past me, but I didn't see any of them exchange greetings. New York is at least twice as big as Paris; and even so, toward the end of February, I met Greta Garbo twice in a week—both times on Fifty-seventh Street between Fifth and Sixth Avenues, on the side where there is one piano store next to another. I'd only seen her in the movies before then, but I know it was she, because the passers-by recognized her, too. Shortly after that, on the same day that I saw Greta Garbo the second time, Richard Horvath came toward me.

"I board a ship in Portugal, and there you're standing," he said. "I take a plane from Hollywood to New York, and the first thing I see on the street is you coming toward me. Are you everywhere?"

"It seems so. Have you left Hollywood?"

"Only for a week. My studio sent me here. For some

conferences. I'm designing the costumes for a new picture. You look well."

"Thanks."

"I heard in Hollywood that you were sick."

"In Hollywood? Who do I know in Hollywood?"

"A pretty girl," he said, winking.

I pretended, rather unsuccessfully, to be surprised.

"A pretty girl?"

He laid a patronizing hand on my shoulder.

"I met that girl who was on the boat with you. I don't know her name. I have a rotten memory for names."

"Oh, *she's* the one you met? I . . . just met her on the train . . . on the way to Genoa . . . she traveled on the *Rex*, too . . . she stayed here a few days . . . then she went on."

"Pretty girl," he repeated stubbornly.

"Yes," I said, as if I were just too polite to contradict him.

"A perfect nose and perfect legs," Horvath said, fastening on the subject unpleasantly. "I'm speaking as an artist. Two things which are rarely perfect in women. Nose and legs. I saw her dance."

"In a studio?"

"No."

"On the stage?"

"No. In a night club where I go every evening. She was a guest there, too, and she was dancing. With a Hungarian fellow. Supposed to be a screen writer. I've forgotten his name, too."

He bent close to my ear, in mock secrecy.

"There was a bit of a scandal about them."

"Scandal?"

"Just a little one. About so big." He demonstrated with his thumb and forefinger how small the scandal was. "In Hollywood nobody even notices things like that."

"Scandal?"

He smiled. There was something patronizing about the smile, too. I didn't like it.

"In which of them are you interested?" he asked. "The girl or the fellow?"

"Neither. Or rather . . . both. Simply because they're Hungarians."

"It's really not very interesting. A very minor scandal. This screen writer and the girl were sitting near the entrance, and dancing together quite a lot. I was dancing, too, and I recalled seeing the girl somewhere before, but I only realized where when she was nice enough to smile at me on the dance floor. She spoke to me, too. She mentioned the boat and you. So I asked her where you were, and whether you were all right. She said you were in New York and that you'd been sick, but were better now. How about going into this cafeteria? I can't get over that Central European habit—coffee at five, with milk and rolls."

We went in and had coffee, and he began telling me about his new movie—in great detail. About the sets, and even more about the costumes, which he had designed. It made me nervous.

"You've aroused my curiosity—about my fellow passengers and their scandal now," I said. "Please—go on with it."

"Was the man one of your fellow passengers, too?"

"And yours. We came on the same boat, you know. But he was seasick. In bed the whole time."

"Was she his girl? Were they traveling together?"

I had to lie.

"Possibly," I said. "I wouldn't know."

"It seemed to me at the time . . . on the boat, she acted as if she were your girl. But in Hollywood, I saw I was mistaken."

I began to be impatient.

"They were sitting near the entrance," I said. "That's how you began the story about the scandal."

"Oh, yes. They were dancing together—what they call 'sexy' dancing. I don't like that sort of thing. Public sensuality disgusts me. But they both dance well. The girl really magnificently. Then a young man, who was drunk, danced with her . . . supposed to be a Russian movie actor . . . handsome fellow. Later I saw the Russian sit down at their table. The three of them were sitting together, drinking and chatting. I was sitting fairly far from them. There wasn't a single loud word leading up to the scene. But suddenly the Hungarian movie fellow smashed his fist into the Russian's face. The Russian hit back. People at the near-by tables were laughing, because the two of them just sat there for quite a while, punching each other in the face, without standing up. But afterward they jumped up and began having a nasty fight. While they were fighting, they fell over some people sitting at a near-by table. So those people began swinging at both of them. So the waiters threw the two of them out in the street. The music never stopped for a second, or the dancing, either. There wasn't any excitement at all."

"And the girl?"

"She went on sitting at the table, alone. She hadn't moved. I was sorry for her. I went over and asked if I couldn't be of some help. She said she didn't dare leave; she was sitting there at the table because the check hadn't been paid. She had been waiting for her friend, but he hadn't come back. Or the other one, either. She had no money with her. I paid the check and asked if I could see her home. She said she didn't want to go home, because she was too angry at her friend. That's how I found out she was living with him. She said she wanted to go to a hotel. So I took her to a hotel in my car and gave her a couple of dollars. I haven't seen her since."

He grinned at me, oddly.

"Your name came up on the way, in the car."

"Really?" I said, trying not to display any interest.

"She said you were the cause of what happened at the night club."

"I?" I said, trying to show great surprise.

"That's what she said. I asked her how anything that happened in Hollywood could be connected with you in New York. She said, oh, yes you were the cause. But she wouldn't say any more."

"And why did they hit each other?"

"Because the Russian was drunk, and made the girl
a proposition while he was dancing with her."

"And the girl told her friend?"

"No."

Again Horvath looked at me strangely. He said, "I'm
just beginning to see the thing clearly. Just since I
met you."

That annoyed me.

"Why did they hit each other?" I repeated.

"I only know what the girl told me. The Russian
made the girl a proposition while they were dancing,
and she turned him down. Then the Russian asked
whether she had refused him because she was the mistress of the man she was with. The girl seems to have
been a little tight, too. She said, yes, she was the man's
mistress, but she didn't love him. So the Russian asked
her why she lived with him, if she didn't love him.
Was he rich? The girl said, no, he was poor, all he had
was debts. The Russian went on pestering the girl with
questions. If she didn't love him and he had no money,
why was she his mistress? The girl said the man she
loved was in New York. He didn't want her. He threw
her at this young fellow's head. So then the Russian
asked in amazement what that meant—one person
throwing her at another. He asked how it happened
that one person could just throw her at another like
that. Then the girl answered that this man she meant
in New York could do even *that* to her. He could do
anything to her."

Horvath smiled again. I was frightfully disconcerted. "Why did they hit each other?" I said again, stupidly.

"Because, at the table, the drunken Russian repeated the whole conversation word for word, just as I've told it to you, to the Hungarian fellow. Whereupon the Hungarian punched him on the chin, which is easy to understand. That's why they fought. As I told you, the girl told me the whole thing in the car while I was driving her to the hotel. We stood in front of the hotel until she finished the story. At the end she cried a little, too, which always makes me less sympathetic, somehow. I dislike that sort of thing. It disgusts me to see a woman crying for love. Please, don't mind . . ."

"Oh, that's all right."

"And don't mind my telling it all in such detail. But—I was dumfounded by—what shall I call it?—the capriciousness of fate or the smallness of the world. To hear this from the girl only a few days ago, and now to get off a plane in New York, and bump into you on the street. You of all people."

The hotel on Long Island, where I went to recuperate at the doctor's advice, was several hours out of New York, a charming little house, on a low hill, with windows facing the ocean. The false spring of late February and early March was even lovelier here. Near the hotel was a miniature village, made up of a grocery, post office, and drugstore, all on one street—as neat and pretty as if it had been built by a movie studio for a picture. My favorite hour of the day was breakfast in the sunny, glassed-in dining room. I sat at a little table next to a huge window through which you could look, between the branches of the bare trees and bushes, far out to sea. Facing me, at the next window, was a little table exactly like mine. The first morning, a middle-aged lady of distinguished appearance sat there having breakfast at the same time as I. She was Mrs. Hilda Cole. The first day that we sat across from each other, I took no notice of her. But the next morning, even though I didn't know whether it was customary in America, I bowed courteously, though not too cordially, as I passed her table. She responded with an automatic smile and went on eating. I sat down, drank my coffee, and read my paper. The next day she was there before me again. When I came in, she smiled first. The fourth day, she came in after me.

I greeted her, and she sat down and called over to me. "Nice morning, isn't it?"

"Very nice," I said with a polite smile.

"We've had good luck with the weather altogether," she said. "Lovely warm weather. And sunshine."

She increased the sunshine by a broad, friendly smile—one for me and one for the waitress who brought her breakfast. The waitress smiled, too. A springlike day in America is full of smiles.

"Beautiful," she said, gazing out at the ocean. "I feel entirely well after just a couple of days here."

"You were sick?"

"Yes, the doctor sent me here."

"Cold?"

"A bad one."

I guessed that she was about forty-eight or fifty. She could still be called an attractive woman. She wore her dark hair parted in the middle, and she had a pale complexion. At moments she had a Madonna-like quality, reminiscent of Italian Renaissance paintings. There were very few people at the hotel. Perhaps that was why, several days before, I had asked the girl at the desk the name of two or three of the guests. That's how I had learned Hilda Cole's name, that she had a lingerie shop on Fifty-seventh Street, and that her clientele were all very rich women. She spent her summer vacation at this hotel every year. She'd spent these few days here so early this year because she'd been sick, but that was unusual.

The next day when I came back from my afternoon walk, I didn't go into the hotel by the main entrance; instead, I walked toward the gate at the back, because the hotel stood on a little hill and there were steps leading up to this gate. And according to Dr. Knopfler's instructions, I had to climb thirty or forty steps slowly every day. It was part of my cure. When I had reached the gate at the top, a voice called up to me from below.

"You shouldn't climb such steep stairs."

I turned and looked down. It was Mrs. Hilda Cole. She came slowly up the steps, too.

"Good morning," I said. "Why shouldn't I climb stairs?"

"Because . . . I've seen the medicine you take every morning after breakfast."

I didn't know what to say.

"I had no idea you had noticed me," I stammered.

Surprisingly, she reached up and put her hand on my arm.

"I recognized those little green pills."

"Do you take them, too?"

"No, but my father took them for years. Digitalis. A wonderful drug."

"Wonderful," I said.

"Digitalis," she said again. She reached the top, and stopped beside me. "These are very steep stairs," she said.

"Thanks for your kindness," I said, somewhat disconcerted, and started to go on into the hotel.

"I hope you don't mind my interfering," she said. "If I hadn't seen those pills on the table, we would probably never have spoken to each other at all. But . . . the thing I like best is to take care of people. I'm a born nurse. I even took a course in nursing. And got a diploma. My mother and I prolonged my father's life ten years."

Again I didn't know what to say. In both Paris and Venice I'd had Americans who didn't know me address me in this friendly, unrestrained, almost intimate way, as though we had known each other for years. I'm one of those Europeans whom the custom delights. There are some who don't like it. Frenchmen like it. Germans don't.

"You're a foreigner?" Mrs. Cole asked me.

"Yes."

"You do have a slight accent."

"A very heavy one, I'm afraid."

"Where do you come from?"

"Hungary."

"I have a Hungarian milliner. She's wonderful. But . . . I don't know exactly where Hungary is."

I flushed. I felt the warmth rise to my cheeks, just like the time on the Italian border when the Fascist officer asked me my religion. All my life I had been a little hurt because so few people in the outside world knew where my country was. It's hard to explain that feeling to Americans, because they can't imagine such a situation. Such a thing could never happen to them. Everybody knows where America is.

"Have I offended you?" Two big brown eyes regarded me anxiously.

"Oh, no. Not at all."

"I'm so sorry," she said.

"But, for heaven's sake, you can't really believe you've offended me? On the contrary, you've been extremely nice to me."

"You're a dear," she said.

"No, I'm not. I may be anything else, but I'm not a dear."

That's how I came to know Mrs. Hilda Cole. The

fact that this woman, who didn't know me at all, left her hand in mine so long made a distinct impression on me—she, a well-dressed lady with a distinguished manner, whom you could describe, without exaggeration, as being decorative, and I, an unknown man of fifty-two! The next morning she sat down at my table, and from then on we ate breakfast together at my table every day.

I saw something of a bond in the fact that, because of her father, she understood my condition as well as a doctor. From time to time, she gently pointed out lapses in my diet. She often went walking with me, and slowed me down when I hurried. She checked the length of our walks on her watch. I must admit that she not only sympathized with me; she actually nursed me. By the end of the first week I was asking myself if the woman wasn't in love with me. She was acting suspiciously like it—I was sure of that. I'm not the man to overestimate the meaning of a woman's glances. But, since Edith, I'd understood that special look which men who are experts on women don't misunderstand. I'd been slow in learning the meaning of the little changes in a woman's expression, but now at last I was beginning to understand them. Our conversations usually consisted of her talking and my listening and making a remark now and then to keep it from being a monologue. But apparently all my comments pleased her.

"I like a man who can listen to a woman, no matter how much she talks," she said.

Trying to recall it all distinctly now, it seems to me that the first deep impression she made on me was the fact that her light, superficial conversation was almost unnoticeably building up to a declaration of her love for me, even to a proposal of marriage. I haven't heard many declarations of love in my life; in fact, I admit I've heard very few. But I've never heard—or read in literature—a more effective avowal than the one Hilda Cole made to me. It took her two or three days to build up this structure out of our conversations—very practically, without a single emotional or poetic word. It was a brand-new method of love-making. Prescribed for men in their fifties. Even today, I think of Hilda Cole with admiration for this. What I call a proposal of marriage, built up out of avowals of love, began when, standing on that steep flight of stairs, she said, "The thing I like best is to take care of people. I'm a born nurse." Could anyone make a cleverer approach to a sick man who was afraid of burdening other people with his illness? Then one evening—it was raining and we were listening to the radio in the hotel lobby—she began to talk about her business. She asked my advice, as a friend, about some banking matter or other, but only in order to bring the conversation around to the fact that she had a little house in New York with two apartments; she lived alone on the first floor; the second was rented to a quiet, married couple. It was also a way of mentioning that the apartment was too big for her and that she sometimes felt very lonesome in it.

Her lingerie business got along so well now, even without her, she said, that her presence wasn't as necessary as it had once been, and she'd love to spend her evenings in her friendly little home—if only there were someone with whom she would enjoy spending them.

"Get married again?" she asked herself with a bitter little smile. "I'm too fussy."

I looked down at the rug in embarrassment. Funny, but I felt like an inexperienced little girl into whose ear an experienced Lothario is softly humming his tune.

"I'm forty-eight," she said. "I'd be horrified if any man made much of having a sexual relation with me."

I realized clearly enough that, strange as it may sound, this was intended as a seduction. She was thinking of her digitalis-fed father whom the doctor had undoubtedly given the same strict orders about his sex life that Dr. Knopfler had given me. I found it moving that any woman should try to make herself desirable to a man who had heart trouble by such a frightful speech. The way in which Juliet confessed to Romeo that she wanted to be his was far more beautiful. But she wasn't the least bit cleverer, or more honest, or more admirable than this realistic lingerie-shop keeper. As I said, I was delighted with her. I paid homage to those American virtues of decency, realism, and sincerity in her, though it is possible they were just her own personal characteristics. (I'm not just grateful to America; I'm prejudiced in its favor. I often say that you can recognize the foreigner who really loves America by the fact that he generalizes the virtues he sees here, and attributes the vices to the individual.)

One morning, a few days later, we were lying on two deck chairs, pushed close together on the sunny beach, when the bellboy brought us our mail. I only had one letter, a thick envelope from Budapest with my lawyer's address printed on it. My fifteen-year-old divorce papers had arrived. I opened the envelope and took out the papers. This was a matter ended and forgotten fifteen years before. But here were these newly arrived, red-sealed documents, translated into English and notarized—and, holding them in my hand, it seemed as if I had only attained my freedom that morning.

Mrs. Cole must have noticed something in my expression, because she said, "Good news?"

"Yes," I said.

"Very good?"

"Very good," I said, looking at her—and I think that was the moment I decided to marry her. A fresh little breeze was blowing from the sea, in the sweet sunshine. With my ticket of freedom in my pocket, I felt ten years younger, sitting there beside this person who held the promise of a peaceful future. When Edith told me to marry, she said I ought to marry an American woman suitable to my age—quiet, serious, decorative— let's say, a widow. Mrs. Cole was lying, with her eyes closed, in the deck chair beside me, and letting the spring sunlight fall on her face. I took a good look at her, surveyed her carefully, without her noticing it. Is she suitable to my age? Yes. Is she quiet, serious? Yes. Decorative? Yes. She's even a widow. Today when there are so many divorced women, widows have a certain standing. A moral superiority over the others. It wasn't such an extraordinary coincidence that everything fitted so completely with Edith's prescription, I thought. The type she described is common in America. Even in Europe I'd heard that America was controlled by widows. There was no other solution for me but Mrs. Hilda Cole.

I looked at her until she opened her eyes.

"You know," she said, "we could have dinner together at Dick's Inn this evening."

"Fine," I said, in high good humor. "I'd love to."

That evening I sat beside her in her little car, as she drove along the shore road to Dick's Inn.

"For days I've been wanting to ask you to go on an outing like this," she said.

"Why didn't you say so?"

"I didn't have the nerve. You never showed before that you'd care at all to spend an evening alone with me . . . anywhere away from the hotel."

"And today I did?"

She nodded her head to indicate that I had showed it, I had certainly showed it—and laughed.

"When?"

I really didn't know when.

"When you looked at me all that time this morning . . . on the beach . . . when you thought my eyes were shut and I didn't notice you were watching me."

I felt again like the little girl with the Lothario. But this competence of hers made me feel good. It gave me a sense of security to have such an experienced friend in my infinite loneliness in this foreign land. That's what I needed now more than anything else.

At Dick's Inn they served a mixed salad in a large wooden bowl. It was the specialty of the house. But this time Hilda mixed it in the kitchen herself, without salt, but in some way which made it very tasty, anyhow. With this observation of my saltless diet, she began her motherly care.

On the way back, I sat silently beside her in the car. It pleased me that she drove so well. Really good women drivers please me. I can't explain, but I have a feeling that certain women have a sixth sense for fast but safe driving which men don't have.

Our headlights shone in rapid succession on two pairs of lovers in the scanty shrubbery by the side of the road. Both couples conducted themselves heroically in the glare of the headlights; neither stopped kissing. We didn't mention them. Then Hilda Cole slowed the car down and we stopped at the side of the road. She got out.

"Wouldn't you like to take a little walk?"

"Yes."

I got out, too.

"How long did you walk today?" she asked.

"Half an hour short of the prescribed amount."

A gentle surf was washing over the beach's edge.

"Take my arm," she said.

I took her arm. She rested her head on my shoulder, according to the rules.

"Do you like to go walking . . . like this . . . with a woman?"

"With you I do."

"Have you gone walking with lots of women?"

"No."

"Are you lying to me?"

"It makes me feel good to have you think I'm lying."

"Why?"

"It's flattering. Your taking me for a lady's man."

"How do I know what you did in Europe? You don't look like a man that women would let alone."

"Nevertheless, they let me alone."

"Liar."

She squeezed my arm.

"I can just imagine how you carried on in Europe."

We walked quietly along the edge of the road, where the lights are.

Her head on my shoulder, she said, "These lights— they're the first American lights you see from the ocean—from a ship."

How could Hilda Cole know that at the very moment she wanted to be particularly nice to me, she was rubbing a handful of salt into a still-bleeding wound? A person is tender, clever, tactful in vain; he can't know when he will cause pain, innocently, unknowingly. It was a bad moment, that memory of the instant when we first saw those lights—Edith, Pali, and I. Perhaps the very one next to which we were now standing was the first. You can't blame anyone for that, though. The one who's to blame is the person who goes to Dick's Inn for dinner with a bleeding wound.

We turned back, got into the car, and went on home to the hotel. It had grown cool and windy. The heated hotel lobby felt good to us. She sensed that something had happened, but she didn't know what. She didn't ask, either. The newspapers, which came from New York every evening, were lying on a table—Siegfried Line . . . Maginot . . . Gamelin . . . Daladier . . .

We said good night in the half-darkness, in a corner of the hotel corridor where a side hall branched off from the main hallway. I thought there was something motherly in her look.

"If only you weren't so sad all the time," she said.

"I'm a man condemned to death," I said, still under the influence of the opened wound. "The difference between me and a condemned man waiting in the death cell is that he knows when the end will come and I don't."

I knew this sample of self-pity was in bad taste, but I couldn't help myself; it just slipped out.

She took my hand with a friendly, reproachful little smile.

"What ideas! That's because you're alone too much."

Grateful and touched by this speech, but really more

out of gratitude, I bent to kiss her on the cheek. She moved slightly, so that her face was turned to mine, and raised her head a little. A gesture impossible to misunderstand, and not to be misunderstood. I kissed her tenderly on the mouth. She returned the kiss, a long, chaste kiss, with lips unmoving. And again—but how could she know?—something happened which spoiled that solemn moment. She grasped my head with the same gesture as Edith. Possibly other women do that, too. It wasn't just my particular bad luck. Possibly—probably—all women hold a man's head that way. Several thousand years ago the beautiful Egyptian courtesans reached for men's heads like that. It was not a hot or passionate kiss, but it was a long one—it tasted like the guarantee of a benevolent and peaceful future. I suppose that, in the last analysis, I was rather horrid that night, because, after that kiss, as I walked down the long hallway alone to my room, I was saying to myself that I had the same sense of contentment and security now that I had had when I left the consulate in Nice with the American visa in my pocket. This kiss was a visa, too. A visa for going on living. For staying alive.

Next day we began taking not only breakfast together at my little table, but lunch and dinner, too. And we did that every day from then on. But only for a few days, because Hilda said, with a sigh, that her self-appointed vacation was coming to an end, and she had to get back to New York on account of business. But we'll spend every minute together until then, she said. I decided that when she left I'd go back to New York with her. I'd gotten to the point where I couldn't imagine a single tomorrow without Hilda. The fact that she was a woman played no part in my great attachment to her. The powerful effect she had on me lay in the fact that, when I was with her, I began to have some sense of a future—a sense I'd lost completely since that first heart attack. At that time I wouldn't have dared make plans two weeks in advance. At that time I still thought God punished men who made plans on their own and didn't entrust the future to Him. Now I caught myself beginning a sentence to Hilda with the words, "Next year . . ."

The day before our return to New York the weather was at its loveliest. (The weather is always at its loveliest when you have to leave a place.) At five in the afternoon the sun was still shining, framing the spring clouds in a narrow band of red gold. We were sitting at a roadstand on which there was a sign, "Luncheonette." We were in the habit of sitting there every afternoon, over a cup of coffee.

"Tomorrow we go back to New York," she said, somewhat nervously. "But first I want to tell you something. There's something in my past I don't want you to hear from anyone else. I'd rather tell you myself."

I was disturbed. I wanted Hilda as she was, without her past life, without her past secrets.

"There's gossip going around New York about me," she went on. "Or rather about my dead husband.

There's a malicious rumor that my husband died in jail."

She stopped speaking, as if she were waiting for me to ask her to go on. She was suffering visibly as she told the story.

"Is it so important to talk about it, Hilda?" I said. "And—why talk about it at all?"

"Because it wouldn't surprise me if you got an anonymous letter someday saying my husband had been executed in Sing Sing. There was gossip of that kind, too. I've gone through awful things."

She gave me her hand. I took it, and she went on talking.

"It's all lies. My husband was an unfortunate man, and his friends were crooks. They were to blame for the whole thing. It's true that my husband did do something wrong."

Her hand trembled in mine.

"This is the first time I've talked about it in ages," she said. "That's why my hand's shaking. Hold it good and tight."

She tried to smile, then stopped abruptly.

"Before it got to court, my husband threw himself out of the twentieth-story window of a hotel. It doesn't matter which one. We were living there at the time. I bought my little house with the money he left me. His friends—the crooks who murdered him—tried to drag me into the affair at the time, to get what little money I had. But they didn't manage to wreck me. That's a long time ago. Twelve years. I've been alone ever since. Working."

We didn't speak. Her hand wasn't trembling any more.

"Do you want to know any more about it?" she asked. "If you do, ask me now, because we aren't ever going to talk about it again."

"I have nothing to ask."

She laid the palm of her hand on my lips and held my mouth closed, tenderly.

"You're a dear," she said.

In spite of all her efforts, you could tell that she was very upset. I could guess how much she must have tortured herself, brooding, before she brought herself to make this confession. There was no doubt about it, the woman already thought of me as her lord and master. I didn't hesitate to take her head and press it to my heart, right there on the edge of the road, in view of the passers-by. It was a romantic and senti-mental gesture, but it was real. What I was thinking at the moment was loathsome, though. Now, writing it down, I hate myself because my critical sense, which has soured so many of the joys of my life, was alert even in that touching moment. You should never be-come conceited, I thought. The reason for my sudden conquest wasn't my fascinating personality at all. My success was so easy because Mrs. Hilda Cole was a trifle shopworn. These beautiful silk stockings would be much higher priced if there weren't "a scarcely notice-able defect in the fabric." But that didn't fundamentally change anything. I was holding in my arms a fine, decent, suitable woman who loved me.

Why was I seized that same night by an irresistible impulse to confess—to write Edith a short note informing her that I was going to be married and to whom? There is no explanation for it in what I know of psychology. A doctor would probably call that kind of self-torture masochism. I'm afraid I would have called it that myself if I'd had the courage to go on thinking about it. I sent the letter to Pali's address at the second-rate studio where he was presumably under contract. As soon as the letter had gone, I was sorry I had written it. I was particularly sorry that I had enclosed a snapshot of Hilda's little daughter. Hilda had an adopted daughter, ten years old, who, she told me happily, loved me already. The child was away at school in the country at the time. But she was coming to New York soon for her vacation. Hilda had sent the child all the pictures she had taken of me and some that the colored doorman at the hotel had taken of the two of us together. The child had written a letter saying, "He's awfully good-looking, and he looks nice, too. You be sure to marry him."

Hilda was happy the day she got that letter. I had seen about twenty pictures of the child. She was a pretty little girl with an intelligent face. She looked at me in a friendly way—even from the pictures. I thought how nice it would be for the three of us to sit down to dinner together every evening. They would love me, and I would love them. They'd be surprised at all the things I'd think up to make them both happy. Perhaps there'd be nobody but these two strange people standing with bowed heads beside a grave in the cemetery, when I was lowered into that strange ground. No one, I thought, not even a victim of amnesia, would ever have forgotten human beings as completely as I'd forget Pali and Edith, with the help of these two angels. And I'd forget Europe, too, and my heart trouble, and everything that's past. As the little car rolled smoothly along toward New York, I was almost drunk with the sense of having a future.

I'm deliberately speeding up the story now. I'm skipping a great deal, because it would upset me too much to set down these days of my story in detail. I'm not writing all this to torture myself, but to put my mind at ease—as far as that is possible. So let's pick up the tale again when I went to Buxter's Hotel, after the wedding, to move my trunk to Hilda's. I moved into the ground floor of the little house with her. (As I see it in my meaner moments, this ground floor was another of Hilda's lures. I wasn't supposed to climb many stairs.)

The first morning I was wakened by Hilda coming into my room on tiptoe and quietly pulling up the shades, as a person does who wants to wake you very gently. The March sunlight shone on my bed. Hilda brought with her a refreshing scent of eau de cologne. She shoved a little table up to my bed, and placed on it a breakfast that conformed strictly to my diet. She took my pulse. Then, bending over to kiss me, she whispered in my ear, "You must weigh yourself—before you eat."

In the bathroom she weighed me on brand-new white scales, and wrote down my weight. An unbounded sense of gratitude swept emotionally over me, but the ever-alert meanness in me immediately spoiled even this. I thought, "Now for the first time I understand why so many sick men marry their nurses." While I was having my breakfast, the *New York Times* lay on my bed, looking smooth and freshly pressed, the way papers do early in the day. Everything was fresh and clean and smooth and hopeful in the morning sun. Then a smiling Hilda opened the door for Dr. Knopfler, who had been waiting outside. This was intended as a surprise for me. Hilda wanted the doctor to be my first guest. She went tactfully out. Dr. Knopfler sat down beside my bed.

"A beautiful apartment," he said. "Your wife showed it to me. I had quite a surprise myself. On her bedroom wall, opposite the bed, there's a map of Hungary in a gold frame."

"I know."

"I asked her why. She said it was a punishment. She has to look at it the first and last thing every day, because she once hurt your feelings by not knowing where Hungary was."

I sighed. Dr. Knopfler sighed. It was an extraordinary situation—two men who had drifted here from the banks of the Danube, sitting in the home of a strange American woman—I in bed, he in an easy chair—and we knew that an unimportant red-haired girl had really placed us both here . . . directed us here from three thousand miles away. Crazy men. Crazy women. Crazy, upside-down world. The doctor leaned toward me.

"Have you had any news?" he whispered.

"About what?" I asked, looking as if I didn't know what he meant.

"About Edith."

"No," I said dryly.

"None at all?"

"Not a word."

He was making a mistake, not as a man, but as a doctor, in stirring up memories of the girl just when I had found a way to go on living. But he couldn't help it. Dr. Knopfler had fallen in love with the girl, as everyone who came near her seemed to.

"You're a wise man," he said. "A strong man."

"What do you mean?"

"To run away from her."

"Are you saying that from a medical viewpoint?"

"Ye-e-s. But even if you'd never had any trouble with your heart, I'd still say it."

"You think she's that dangerous?"

"Not to everybody."

"Only to me?"

I might have been mistaken, but it seemed to me

that the doctor blushed slightly. He said, "Let's get on with our business."

With that he took his stethoscope out of his bag.

That was on a Wednesday. On Sunday evening I went to bed at eight, as usual. Hilda and I chatted a bit. She told me her little daughter, Maggie, was coming home from school the next week and would spend a few weeks with us. Hilda opened a capsule of sleeping medicine, and I took the contents in a spoonful of water. The doorbell rang. Hilda went out and came back with a letter. Airmail, special delivery, Beverly Hills, California. The letter was from Pali, and it began with this sentence, "I simply can't find words to express what I've gone through with that deadly little beast who sleeps with me and loves you." Hilda left me alone with the letter. I read it through. As Edith had taught me once in the Hotel Grindale, I took a second sleeping powder, in order to lose consciousness as fast as possible.

CHAPTER THIRTEEN

Tuesday morning I was sitting at the desk, with little Maggie on my lap.

"Please, Mommy, go out a minute," she said to Hilda. "I have something very private to tell him."

I was that "him." "Father" would have been too much, "Mr." too little.

"No," Hilda said, and lifted her from my lap. "Let 'him' alone. Don't you see he wants to write a letter."

"All right," Maggie said. "But later I'm coming back and tell you something. Very important."

"All right, darling."

They went out. The day had been bad from the beginning. There was a dispatch from Vienna in the *New York Times,* in which I read about a new victim to the occupation of Austria—the well-known Viennese lawyer, Dr. Moritz S., had shot his wife and himself. Another thing we were experiencing now for the first time—the horrible feeling of reading two lines like that about people you knew, in a foreign country, in a foreign tongue. Dr. Moritz S. was the brother of a publisher of a liberal newspaper. He had been my sister's lawyer, too. He represented her in a business deal in Vienna once, and I had to confer with him frequently on my sister's behalf. He was a soft-spoken old man, over sixty, and looked like a scholar. In the course of our negotiations, he often said, "No need to be rash or impatient. Things can always be settled nice and slow, without excitement. All you need is patience and a clear head." He used to play up the dispassionate manner of a wise old man a little. And he used to say, "You Hungarians are much too explosive." Now he and his wheezing, gray-haired wife lay here on the desk in front of me, in the *New York Times*—dead. His name printed in an American paper affected me like the epitaph on a tombstone. I could hear his soft voice again, "You Hungarians are much too explosive." I couldn't imagine the instant when he turned to his sickly old wife and pointed the revolver at her. Did he do that "nice and slow, without excitement" too? This event was a fact, but for me it would continue forever to be a monstrous lie, like so many other things which had happened since 1939.

The letter I was about to answer when Maggie dashed in was from Max Auer in Prague. Max, a young Austrian, was Viennese correspondent for that last paper I worked on, the one that fired me. In Budapest I sometimes took down in shorthand the reports he telephoned from Vienna. Max was a dry, laconic reporter, but this letter of his was delivered in as rhapsodic a style as if it had been written by a condemned man on his last night in the death cell. Nothing but exclamation marks, lamentations, pleas—nothing but superlatives—I must help him get out of Prague and into America. It wasn't like the poor devil's style at all. What could I do for him here, where I was only a tolerated nobody myself? I did the only thing I could. I gave my Budapest lawyer instructions to send Max some money from my account through his Prague representative immediately. There was a postscript to Max's letter. "I hear from Vienna that Mitzi G. and her mother committed suicide by turning on the gas in the kitchen, the day before they were to have been shipped to Poland in a cattle car with sixty other Jewish families." Mitzi G. was a lively Viennese divorcée with a reputation for being well-dressed. I knew her because one of my colleagues wanted to marry her. Mitzi made him very unhappy by not caring for him. Mitzi was a lover of Paris clothes, an adorer of the opera, an attender of first nights. The kind of mondaine who leaves one party in the middle of the night to rush to another. My drab, hard-working colleague was hardly a proper partner for that kind of life. Now Mitzi and her old mother lay on the desk in front of me, in the postscript of a letter—dead. My colleague had emigrated to London at the time, and was still there. Poor Mitzi, she could have gone with him, but she had chosen this way. I stared at the pieces of paper. At the familiar names. They die, end their lives and the lives of those they love as soon as things become unbearable. It's almost a crime that I still have my life, because I managed to escape. Just so that my heart can crack up, wear itself out, destroy itself minute by minute. At instants like this, I feel it isn't enough, that I'm a swindler who, by some clever trick, pays less taxes to history than he owes.

About noon Edith's letter arrived. I knew it would come. I'd been expecting it ever since I'd received Pali's. Her writing me a letter was as little surprise as what she said. Pali had no contract. Pali was starving. He wasn't called Pali Maybaum any more, but Paul Monnier. But he was starving just the same. She had managed, with considerable difficulty, to have a screen test made. It was turned down unanimously. The night clubs couldn't use her as a dancer. There were dancers there who couldn't get contracts, who all danced better than she did at her best. Pali was horrid to her. Pali drank and spent the night with other women. Pali— Paul Monnier—once beat her up. I must rescue her. Her money was going. She didn't want to become a prostitute. I *must* rescue her! She had put aside enough money to come to New York, to me. She always remembered that this sum was tucked away in an envelope, a sacred thing, not to be touched. "I've never loved anyone but you in my life, no one else, and you threw me away because you couldn't believe such a thing was possible. I couldn't believe it either at first. Now I know, but now it's too late." She realized I was sick and she had no right to endanger my life. Even though I was responsible for her unhappiness. She didn't want to upset me if I was happy with my new wife. But I could help her. She wasn't asking for money; she wouldn't have me think so for anything. No money, absolutely no money at all. Just some little job. That's what I should get her—work. Maybe in my wife's shop. We wouldn't have to see each other, perhaps not ever again. "You know how good I am at sewing. I always made my good silk underwear myself. Please rescue me!"

Before dinner there was a light knock on my door. I knew it was little Maggie. I was already familiar with the tap of her little fingers.

"Come in, darling."

She came in and threw her arms around me.

"I want to tell you something. A secret."

I kissed her small healthy face.

"Go ahead. I'm listening."

Ever since I've been a grown man, I've been afraid of what little children wanted to tell me in private. And usually the fear proved to be justified, as it did now. Maggie regarded me seriously. I think she must have been imitating her teacher when she asked the children questions. She began with an unexpected question.

"Have you any money?"

"Yes."

"In the bank?"

"Yes."

"Much?"

"No, not much."

"You didn't marry my mother for her money?"

"No. I have enough of my own."

"Do you love her?"

"Very much."

"Would you mind if I asked you for something?"

"No."

"Could we, please, have another baby—at least one?"

I had known the game would end badly for me. But I hadn't expected to be checkmated in seven moves. I smiled in embarrassment and stroked Maggie's hair.

"You know my best friend, Peg Mayer," she went on, "well . . . she has two sisters already. And they've just had another new baby. They have such a good time. Peg once told me what fun they have every night when they go to bed. I cried about it all day. I'm all alone. I'm so happy now because you married my mommy. Because I know you can only get babies if your husband wants them. I really need a sister, or a brother; it doesn't matter much. In school it's nice— with lots of friends. But at home there ought to be a mother and father and lots of brothers and sisters. Can we have some?"

"That depends on God, Maggie."

She looked at me suspiciously. Fortunately Hilda came in then, and they went to the bathroom to wash their hands for dinner. Through the door I could hear Maggie telling her what she'd been asking me for. Hilda laughed loudly. It was natural enough for her to laugh, but it was disconcerting, anyhow.

No, I wouldn't answer Edith's letter. Just as I hadn't answered Pali's. I had acted toward them both as a strong man—even a cruel one. I must not weaken. Never again. Whatever I wrote to Edith, the correspondence could only end badly for me. There weren't ten words in the entire dictionary which I could put together to make up a clever answer. My old game, "If I had a million dollars," again. If I had a million dollars, I'd send this letter of Edith's to Bernard Shaw, who, I think, is the greatest writer in the world. I'd enclose a check for $100,000, and ask him to draw up a short answer to her letter, from which it wouldn't appear that I loved her or longed for her, or that I was angry at her or hated her. In which nothing would be apparent except that she shouldn't come. And all this in a manner which wouldn't hurt her feelings and wouldn't reveal mine. But that's only a silly daydream. Simply don't answer. I have put my wounded, short-lasting life in order, my last days, as the saying goes. It mustn't be upset now. I know that I'm far less cruel than I acted the time I "threw" Edith away. I know that the fear of death was more powerful in me then than the desire to go on living with her. But now it's too late to try to give her a better opinion of me. Too late and too dangerous. If I gave in even a hair's breadth now, it wouldn't only be dastardly toward my wife; it would also be suicide.

It would be best to destroy her letter now. Then the complicated, new four-line address, which was written on the back, would be lost, and I couldn't answer even if I wanted to. But I knew myself. The minute I burned the letter, I'd be seized with an irresistible urge to write to her. The motor which once moved the reporter in me would begin to turn again. I'd begin to make ingenious inquiries, to telephone, telegraph.

Play detective, go to a private detective agency. The hunt would grow madder and madder until I'd found her. When I was a reporter, I often did that sort of thing for my paper. Hunted up impossible addresses, found people who were in hiding, for whom even the police had searched in vain. By the time I'd discovered her address in that way, the hunt would have stirred me up to such an extent that I would surely write her some sort of impassioned nonsense. I must not destroy her letter. There was a much simpler solution. I must write to her now, while I was still capable of thinking coolly. "Things can always be settled nice and slow, without excitement," poor Dr. Moritz S. had said. I must write her a short note, just a few words. Write to her quietly, impersonally. She mustn't come near us. Then, quite apart from my reply, I'd tactfully see that she got some money. Or find some sort of position for her. Perhaps with Dr. Knopfler's help. I had to help her. And I would. But no further contact at all, if life was dear to me.

"You're nervous," my wife said at dinner.

Edith's letter in my pocket made me feel guilty. I was frightfully uncomfortable, because now I had to deceive this woman and this child.

"I got a letter today," I said.

"From Europe?"

Her question made it easier to lie.

"Yes. From Switzerland."

"What did it say?"

"They're afraid. Of the Germans in the north, and

the French in the west. It's not impossible that the great clash will take place on Swiss soil. I heard them saying that every day, as long ago as last autumn, in the coffeehouses in Geneva."

It troubled my conscience to use this horror, this war, to camouflage my little private drama. But I was so restless by now that I could only have spoken in a nervous, overwrought tone—and the only suitable and natural text for such a tone was a conversation about the war.

"General Gamelin will defeat them," I said, my voice trembling noticeably. "Not in Switzerland. I think he'll attack Italy from Savoy. The French army has the best artillery in the world. And the Alpine infantry, the *chasseurs alpins*—they're superb soldiers. Gamelin was a *chasseur alpin* himself when he was young."

My miserable state of mind made a good actor of me.

"How good that you got away," Hilda said.

My voice was still shaking.

"The letter said that my friends . . . who stayed there . . . are very nervous now. They'd like to come here. But they can't get visas."

Hilda the dear, looked at me for a long time. I could tell from her glance that she wanted to say, "Very strange you're that upset about people in neutral Switzerland." But it was undoubtedly just my bad conscience saying it. Her long, penetrating gaze showed pure affectionate concern, nothing more.

Next morning when Hilda went to work, I sat down

to write to Edith. I sat down intending to write to her that she must absolutely not come near me. It could hardly be a shock to her. It would seem quite natural after two such cruel acts as my packing her off to Holly- wood and my letting her know I was married. Twice I'd acted like an executioner. Now I must remain in the role, and bear all the self-reproach and contempt bound up with the hangman's profession. A senti- mental hangman would be such a perverse phenome- non that he ought to be killed himself.

And in this spirit, I began writing the letter. "Dear Edith, My answer is no, no, no."

But . . . I said to myself, I haven't any right to wound her again on top of everything else. So I fol- lowed this short, harsh statement with a sentence, a conciliatory sentence, just to take the sharp edge off those three no's. I started to explain to her in detail that it wasn't my intention to hurt her again. So my letter began to grow longer, and that in itself weakened the rebuff so much that sentences began to appear in which there was a slight overtone of encouragement. I went on writing more and more feverishly and elabor- ately. The letter began to carry me along, to hurtle me along like brakes giving out on a downgrade. I noticed with alarm how the rejection was slowly turn- ing into a veiled invitation. When I noticed this, I calmed myself immediately by telling myself that everything was all right, I wouldn't mail the letter, anyhow. There's only a little more to say, and I'll finish up this little bit *just for myself,* to unburden myself.

I made up a definition. "A letter isn't a letter until you put it into the mailbox."

Obviously. Up to then, it's only a piece of paper with writing on it. "Not a letter yet"—this formulation freed me, released all the brakes in me. It's an age-old experience, a kind of pacifier, "writing it all out." Before the discovery of bromides and barbiturate preparations this was the best sedative. It's not the mailing of the letter that's relaxing, but the writing. Too bad I didn't remember this old remedy sooner. I could have relieved my mind oftener without the druggist's aid.

I had already covered ten closely written pages with my frankest, most painful thoughts—even those I had never before admitted to myself. It was a marvelous relief. And it was marvelous to know that the more reckless and forbidden the revelations I wrote down, the more certain it was that these sheets of paper would never be a posted letter. Well, then, no restraint. *Postscript:* "Come at once, at once! Leave the instant you read this!"

I put the letter into an envelope and sealed the envelope. That in itself wouldn't send the letter on its way. I wrote the address on the envelope. Like a child, I was playing with fire. I put on an air-mail stamp. That wouldn't send it on its way either, that wouldn't change it into a letter. I went for a stroll down the block, the letter in my pocket. The words kept going around in my head, "My pocket's a safe place for it. It can't fly away from there and land itself in a mailbox." Even so, for safety's sake I kept my hand pressed down on my pocket, and smiled at the thought that I was playing like a child. I walked and walked. I came to a crossing. Stopped, waiting for the green light. Then I crossed carefully. On the way I was thinking, "If an auto ran me over at one of these crossings, they'd pick me up unconscious, telephone for an ambulance, a policeman would go through my pockets to find out who I was, and either he or someone else would kindheartedly put the stamped and addressed letter into a mailbox . . . then I'd be brought back to health in a hospital . . . and . . ." It wasn't a game any more. This walking daydream slowly became an obsession. And as a matter of fact, a taxi did almost run over me. I turned to go home. Somewhere I stopped at the edge of the sidewalk, in front of a mailbox, and (there was no question of temporary insanity—I hadn't gone crazy at all) quietly, coldly as a hangman, I dropped the letter into the mailbox.

I say, "hangman." As I've said, the word had gone around in my head often that day. Now, at the moment when the letter disappeared into the opening, and I stared after it, the word "hangman" touched off a grotesque picture in my mind. A hangman who leads the condemned prisoner to the gallows and then suddenly hangs himself. Because that's what I had done.

Late that evening, after dinner, when Maggie was already in bed, my wife and I sat talking at the table. It had reached the point now where I no longer spoke an honest word. I wasn't myself. An actor was sitting there with the woman, a perfect actor.

"I got a letter today," I said, and recklessly threw Edith's letter, which was written in Hungarian, on the table. "Annoying."

Hilda glanced at the paper and shoved it back.

"Is it in Hungarian?"

"Yes."

"Who from?"

"A girl. Hungarian, too. She writes that she'd like to come to New York. She claims that she knows me."

"And you don't know her?"

"Perhaps. I remember the name. Gaal. I knew someone by that name in Budapest. If I'm not mistaken, he had daughters."

"What does she want of you?"

I shrugged my shoulders.

"Work. As a matter of fact . . . she writes . . . that she'd like me to get her a job in your business. Fantastic how refugees three thousand miles away find everything out. Our address . . . that I'm married . . . what kind of business you have . . . everything."

"Don't get upset about it. The poor souls always try everything."

"I don't know if I should even answer her."

"Why, you wicked man," Hilda said.

"I don't even know her. How can I vouch for her?"

"One seamstress more or less doesn't matter to me," she said.

"But if she's no good."

"Any young thing can learn that kind of sewing," Hilda said. "I'll take her under my wing . . . because she's a countrywoman of yours. Because she's Hungarian, and . . . Hungary is situated on the Danube, south of Poland and north of Yugoslavia. I know now."

The playacting was getting harder for me all the time.

"You're kindheartedness itself," I said.

"Write to her to come."

"You're too kind," I said. "Americans are too kind and trusting. We're more cautious about strangers."

"Write to her. We'll see soon enough. Nowadays you have to help everyone. Don't worry about me."

As if I were doing her a favor, I said, "All right. Perhaps I'll write tomorrow."

"Not *perhaps*. You must write her without fail."

"All right."

"Promise?"

"I promise."

The letter had long since been flying over the clouds, toward the west. I couldn't look her in the eye. I stood up, went slowly to the window, and looked automatically up at the dark, starless sky.

CHAPTER FOURTEEN

Edith arrived in New York. I found it out when my wife came into the room one evening and said, "The red head turned up this morning."

I let the newspaper I was reading sink into my lap. I had become an actor again. I pretended not to understand what she was talking about.

"Red head?"

"The Hungarian girl."

"Oh? She has red hair?"

"Yes. Didn't you ever see her?"

"Maybe in Budapest . . . in passing. Well?"

"I took her on, of course. She began work this afternoon."

She liked Edith, I could tell.

"She's not at all pretty, but there's something attractive about her," she said. "She has a saucy little nose, but it suits her face. And she's awfully skillful."

"I'm glad. It was nice of you to take her on."

I went on looking at the paper, as if that interested me more. Hilda was standing in front of the mirror, taking off her hat.

"If you'd like to see her . . ." she said.

"I will. Sometime when I call for you."

Edith is behaving cleverly, I thought. As long as I

don't go there, she won't turn up, either. At that moment we were acting like two ingenious criminals who plan a burglary or a murder without being in contact with each other. Or like two who have already committed a crime.

The next day, I felt it was too soon to go there. Not every day, but two or three times a week, I called for Hilda at work a little before six, and we walked home together. I had been due to call for her for several days, so the next day I really should have gone. But, as I say, it was too soon. I didn't want to see Edith yet, sitting there sewing among the other working girls. By five I began to be very nervous and was on the point of leaving. No. No. If only because Hilda mustn't think I was curious about the girl. About five I went to a movie. I settled myself in the center of a row to make getting out harder. And I didn't leave. There was a girl in the picture who walked like Edith. There was a woman in the picture who had a hat like Hilda's. There was a young man in the picture who, from the back, looked like Pali. And a French headwaiter shaved off his mustache in the picture just as I had years before. I found out long ago that if you're in an emotional spot, every movie seems to be about yourself. I stayed there until six-thirty. When I came out, it was pouring.

"It was very sensible of you not to call for me," Hilda said when she came in a few minutes after I did. "It's awful out. Rainy and windy."

She went out, changed her things, and came back.

"She was very smart today, too," she said.

"The Hungarian girl?"

"Yes. And I was going to teach *her*. She sews better than I do."

I escaped into my newspaper again. Then I delivered a long lecture on the relations of England, Belgium, and Holland. I missed little Maggie, who'd gone back to school a few days before; playing and joking with her would have been a better camouflage than reading the paper and delivering hypocritical speeches on international politics, in which my only interest was that they should last long. I broke off abruptly because Hilda was listening, respectful and intent, not suspecting that I was only talking because I was afraid of giving myself away. I felt I was putting it over, but it made me unhappy. Sooner or later the situation must become untenable.

The third day I went to the shop before six to call for Hilda. I couldn't put it off any longer. As I went in, I decided that if the act didn't go over, and Hilda noticed anything, I'd tell her everything tonight at home, like a child telling its mother. I'd send Edith money, and Hilda would let her go, and the whole thing would be over, once and for all. I was beginning to discover that acting is a difficult profession, particularly if you're not an actor.

In the front room, Hilda was showing a dignified, elderly lady some pale, peach-colored silk. I knew who the woman was. A very wealthy woman, one of the mainstays of Hilda's business. I didn't go near them. I walked slowly toward the open door that led to the workroom. I stopped in the doorway and looked in. Edith was sitting among the other girls at a long table. She was embroidering something. She was talking to her neighbor in French, but I couldn't hear what they were saying. Her ill-fated adventure had left its marks on her face. And also the fact that she had lived with a man. Or is it possible that I only imagined you could tell about the man?

As usual, I said hello to all the girls at once. Edith answered with the others.

"Good evening."

And sank back into her work, as if to indicate, "All right. I understand. It shall be just as you wish. We'll act as though we didn't know each other." A minute later the millionaire customer left, and my wife came into the workroom. Because of Hilda, I had to go over now and shake hands with the girl.

"Miss Gaal?" I asked.

"Yes."

"Now that I see you, I do remember you. How are you?"

She blushed, stood up, and said respectfully, "I'm fine, thank you. And I'm so grateful to you for helping me."

"Don't mention it."

My wife was watching us with a broad, happy smile, with the satisfaction of a benefactor. Again I was very troubled at being such a perfect actor. How much longer could I endure this new profession? Not long, I felt. Certainly not long.

I didn't know anything about Edith, where she was living, with whom—if it was a man—nothing. I wasn't conscious of any desire to know more about her. I wasn't jealous. What could that mean? Was I cured? No. But . . . it was so clear that she was alone in the world, and waiting for me. I made no plans. I gave myself over to my fate; let it do with me what it willed. I would "will" to no end, will as I would. I hadn't "willed" to write the letter. I hadn't "willed" to put it into the mailbox. I hadn't "willed" constantly to deceive my wife, either. As far as my life was concerned, it was apparently only Edith who "willed" anything. Things just happened to me. Edith was not a human being. Edith was what men called a witch in the Middle Ages. This perception of my helplessness made me almost calm.

Two days later, when I called for my wife at work again, I had nearly arrived at a firm decision. It couldn't go on like this any longer. This evening I would tell Hilda everything. I would unburden myself. She's good and she's wise. That rare type to whom you can tell everything—and only good will come of it. This unfortunate situation would come to an end.

It was after six when I came into the shop. Hilda was sitting at a table with a bookkeeper, and they were both puzzling over some tax forms. The day's work was over. The girls were getting on their things and going home. The door to the outer hall was open. One by one, the girls went through the door into the hall and toward the elevator. I gestured smilingly to my wife that she shouldn't disturb herself, I'd wait until she was through. I walked slowly up and down. The girls were going, still going out toward the corridor. Edith went out, too, with the French girl. My wife was writing figures on a sheet of paper. The bookkeeper was filling out a form. I walked up and down the big room, then wandered out into the corridor, and came slowly back into the room again through the open door. Then slowly out into the hall again. A bunch of girls were standing, waiting for the elevator. I walked slowly up to the elevator. I didn't know why. My unconscious knew, but it didn't tell me. Then I waited with the girls until the elevator came and the door opened. The girls crowded into the elevator. Edith went with them. The French girl went, too. I went, too. The elevator man shoved the door closed behind us, and we sank down into the depths. There were only three stories, but I had the feeling that I had started on my way to a depth of ten thousand stories. But I was absolutely calm; there was even a kind of serenity flowing over my nerves. At the ground floor I pushed my way out of the elevator with the girls in the most matter-of-fact way. Out in the street, in front of the entrance, the girls turned off in different directions. Some went right, some left. Edith went left to the next corner with the French girl who had been sitting beside her in the workroom the other day. She was a delicately built little brunette. I joined them, which Edith didn't seem to find surprising; at least she acted as if it were perfectly natural. We walked three abreast, I on the left,

Edith in the middle, her friend to the right. Her friend went on talking.

"And in the same place they wanted six dollars for a pair of perfectly plain brown shoes," she said. "That's too much, don't you think?"

"Not really," Edith said. She turned to me. "Do you think that's much?"

"It depends on what kind of shoes they were," I said.

I put both my hands in my pockets, because they were shaking so. We stood on the corner, at the bus stop, where a few other people were waiting for the bus, too. There was a beautiful rose-colored sunset.

"I'd like you to meet Fernande Batault," Edith said.

Fernande Batault smiled at me and held out her hand. She was a thin little girl. Her nose was a little too big, and her eyes were very black in her pale face. She looked more Italian than French.

"I've seen you often," she said. "You're the boss's husband, aren't you?"

"Yes," Edith answered for me.

We stood waiting.

"She's a lovely woman—our boss," Fernande said. "Fine. A lady. But they say her first husband wasn't much of a gentleman."

Edith gave her a reproachful glance.

"Oh, everybody knows about it," Fernande said. "It was in all the papers." To make everything all right, she added, "But that little girl of hers is an angel."

We got on the bus. I sat beside Edith. We held hands. Fernande sat across from us and didn't seem at all surprised. She accepted it as an old relationship between the two of us about which it was no longer necessary to make any comment. Fernande was a Parisian. For a man to wangle a job for his mistress in his wife's business was a story she'd heard over and over again, nothing more. We got off somewhere in the neighborhood of Greenwich Village. Edith was still holding my hand. She led me along. Fernande took my other arm. Holding each other by the hand, we walked off like three bohemians in Montmartre. Fernande was singing a French song rather loudly, but no one paid any attention to us. Edith acted toward me as if all this had been arranged between us to the last detail long before. I don't suppose any woman in the whole world could have acted more cleverly in such a situation.

Suddenly Fernande stood still.

"Well, what are we going to do about the room?" she asked.

I discovered that they lived in the same block and up to now had had single rooms. This evening they were planning to take a double room together. In the place where Edith was living now—run by a Mrs. Glicksman, who made her living renting rooms.

"It's cheaper and you're not alone," Fernande said. "But what shall we do now?"

This time I didn't wait to find out what Edith "willed."

"We'll do this, Fernande," I said. "You'll take over Edith's room at Mrs. Glicksman's—so that you'll be near us—and we'll take the double room."

"That's fine," Fernande said. She turned to Edith. "Funny you kept this such a secret. But I don't suppose I can blame you. After all, we've only known each other a few days."

We were standing in front of a men's furnishing store.

"But we got to be very fond of each other," Fernande said to me by way of explanation.

I wasn't paying much attention to what she said. I went into the store to buy a pair of pajamas. They showed me a pair in dark blue and one in scarlet red. I selected the red. I came out with the package in my hand, feeling so carefree and gay I could have flown on wings. But just for the hundredth of a second, the doubt flashed through my mind—not for the first time since New Year's Eve—had I gone mad?

CHAPTER FIFTEEN

WE WENT to bed early. There were two beds standing close together in the room. She was lying at my left. She put her head on my chest. For a long time we didn't speak. Then she raised her head.

"I'm going to lie on the other side," she said.

"Why?" I asked her, while she got up and walked around the bed to lie down again on my right side.

"I don't want to rest the weight of my head on your heart."

"That couldn't do any harm," I said. "The doctor told me external pressure wasn't harmful."

"But I hear it beating, and it seems to be accusing me. Every beat sounds as loud in my conscience as in the doctor's stethoscope."

"What a child you are!"

"But a guilty one," she said.

"Why?"

"Because your heart is beating so fast. That's because of me."

"No," I said. "It's because of the Poles and the French, because of the Jews, and Hungary, and Europe. A person may have saved his hide, his bones, all his organs, by crossing the ocean—but not his heart."

"But I did your heart harm. By coming back. Even though you chased me away."

We were silent again, motionless, for a long time. That great, luxuriant bush of red hair was close to my lips and my nose. She seemed to have gotten the habit of sweet-smelling American shampoos. But they couldn't destroy the natural scent of her hair which affected me now just as it once had on the *Rex*.

"Now I'm here," she said low. "When I offered myself to you, you threw me out. Now I'm here—but I'm not as I was then. I'm not a . . ."

I interrupted her.

"Don't try to explain. Why should you? Why bring the matter up at all? Thousands and thousands of men have loved—how shall I put it?—divorced women. And have married them and been happy with them."

"But that's not the first, true, lovely . . . being-together."

"And how many men have loved widows, and married them?"

"But the first day . . . wasn't the true bliss it should be."

"The greatest tragedies of love—murder, suicide—are caused by other men's wives. Who bothers about whether a woman is physically pure nowadays?"

"I do."

She leaned her elbow on the pillow and began to explain.

"I had to give myself to that man."

"Don't torture yourself," I said, "or me, either. Let's forget it."

"No, let's not. When a woman decides to live with a man, to follow a career with him . . . whether she loves him or not, whether she's his wife or not, it's her duty to give herself to him. People don't usually agree about it in advance. It's taken for granted. A gentleman's agreement, shall I call it? Anyhow . . . the thing is . . . when it's a matter of working together, having a career together, living in the same place . . . there's no question of a sexual problem any more. It's part of the friendship, of the common troubles and joys, the common livelihood . . . it's just part of it. The kind of woman who would deny her partner *that*, in my opinion, is stingy and dishonest. I've always loathed women who made a great to-do about it."

"Then why are you making such a fuss about it?"

"Because it will always make me sad."

"What will?"

"That he . . . and not you."

"Why?"

"Because you'll never believe why I did it. Why I accepted such a situation. You'll never believe it. I gave myself to another man so that you wouldn't die."

I wanted to answer, but she covered my mouth with the palm of her hand.

"Don't interrupt," she said. "The moment has come when I have the courage to tell you all this. Perhaps I'll never be so brave again. I did it for the sake of your life. I did it in order to bind myself to another man. I thought he'd never let me come back to you. And that you'd detest me."

She was speaking very loud, almost shouting.

"I wanted to do something which couldn't be undone! I saw you wanted it, too. That's why I went away with him."

"For God's sake," I said, "don't be so upset about it."

"But I am upset about it. Because I can't endure the thought that now you don't believe me . . . and I just talk and talk because I can't talk about anything else now . . . and I haven't the faintest hope that you'll believe me."

She buried her head in the pillow. I placed my hand on her thick red hair—like a priest.

I said, "If your motive was so noble, it shouldn't hurt you so."

The answer came, muffled, from the pillow.

"But it does hurt. And it will hurt. Always."

I lifted her head tenderly and laid it back on my chest.

"Do you know the story of Saint Mary of Egypt?" I asked her.

"No."

"She's a Catholic saint. She was an Egyptian girl, this 'Holy Mary, the Egyptian,' as the old chronicles call her. When she was young she wanted to go 'to adore and worship the holy cross in Jerusalem.' But she was poor. She had no money for the trip. As the ship was setting sail from Egypt with other pilgrims who could pay the fare, Mary went to the mariners and said to them, 'Fair sirs, I have nothing to pay you with, but I abandon my body to you, to do withal your pleasure for my passage.' And they took her on that condition. And Jesus, for whom she did it, loved her."

She thought it over, then she asked softly, "And she's a saint?"

"Yes. God even performed three miracles to bring her to heavenly glory. Shall I tell them to you?"

She was looking at me now with a pleading smile, like a two-year-old child again.

"Please, please, tell me."

"Well, the first miracle was this," I said, in the tone in which one tells a fairy story to a very little child. "Every time this Mary prayed to God, her body rose a foot and a half into the air. The second miracle was that an old monk went to meet her, and saw her on the shore of the river Jordan. But she was standing on the opposite shore. Then Mary made the sign of the cross upon the water, and went on it, and came over to him. And the third miracle was when Mary died on the desert, and the old monk had no spade to bury her, and a lion came and dug a grave for her with his claws."

She listened to the lovely old story, her eyes wide.

"You're not a Catholic," she said, low. "How do you know all this?"

"I used to have an old book at home. *The Golden Legend, or Lives of the Saints*. When I was sick and had to stay in bed, I used to read it."

She thought it over again.

Then, "Poor little Mary," she whispered.

Early in the morning I was wakened by someone knocking on the door.

"Who's there?" Edith called.

"Fernande."

"What do you want, dear?"

"Aren't you coming to work with me?"

"No."

"In case you decide to come, I'll wait for you in the lobby."

"No, dear. I'm not coming."

"Will I see you this evening?"

"We'll be home. Just knock."

"*Au revoir.*"

"*Au revoir.*"

CHAPTER SIXTEEN

Neither of us mentioned the fact that neither she nor I was going back to Hilda. As if there'd never been a shop, as if I'd never had a wife. We started out where we had broken off in Genoa, when we left the train and went to the hotel, and she said to me at the desk in the lobby, "Let's take a double room." That time we took a room together, too, but I left it to her and went to sleep in another room, alone. I remembered it was number 325. We started out where we broke off that night, December 31, 1939, when she said to me, "You don't want to stay in the same room with me?" It took me until March, 1940, to answer in the affirmative. Yes, I wanted to stay in the same room with her. I didn't want anything else in life, in the world.

I didn't communicate with my wife at all. The amazing part was that I took it perfectly for granted—I who always examined my faults so closely. Again my unconscious was better informed than I was. It knew already how short a time this whole adventure would last. So short a time that it wouldn't pay to let my wife know the reasons and what I intended to do. But even so . . . now when I look back on those days, I am frightened by the ease, the naturalness, with which I perpetrated

187

this unkindness to Hilda—by my absolute peace, which cut me off from everything in the world.

In the evening Fernande knocked on the door. She came in. We got dressed. Fernande taught me how to tie my necktie "more youthfully." Then the three of us went out to dinner. So far she hadn't said a word about my wife. Not until Edith said:

"Did she ask about me?"

'No."

"Didn't she look at you strangely? No different from usual?"

"Why should she?"

"She knows we're friends."

"She didn't look at me. But I . . ."

"But you . . . what?"

"I kept out of her way. I didn't look at her all day. Frankly, I'm scared of her. She's such a big, strong, stern woman."

"Were you scared she'd beat you?"

"I wouldn't have cared for that, either. But that wasn't what I was scared of. It's because we're in the wrong."

"Not you. Just the two of us."

"I am, too," Fernande said, like a child asking other children to let her play, too. She wanted to be part of this romantic adventure, even if it was going to end in tragedy. Even then. Perhaps, particularly then! She added, "You couldn't tell a thing from her face. Besides, there were lots of customers today. She wasn't free a minute."

The next evening, Fernande brought a similar report. And a present for me, a navy-blue tie with a design of pink and sky-blue rings intertwined. Edith refused to let me wear it, for which I was grateful. The three of us went to dinner together again. The third evening Fernande rushed into our room, very upset.

"It happened," she said breathlessly. "She asked me questions. She was pale but calm."

Edith grew serious.

"Where did she ask you?"

"In her little office. She sent for me."

"Just for that?"

"No. First she gave me some patterns from a Paris fashionable magazine. Then she began to ask questions. I didn't give anything away. I said I hadn't seen either you or him since you left."

"Did she believe you?"

"No."

"How do you know?"

"By her smile when she finally said, 'You can go now.' "

I poured some rum into a tumbler.

"Are you allowed to do that?" Edith asked.

"Of course. For weeks now," I lied.

"Did Dr. Knopfler say so?"

I gulped down the rum.

"I don't want to hear that name again," I said.

"Why?"

"I don't like him."

Edith poured some rum for herself, too.

"I don't, either," she said.

She drank up the rum.

"An ugly man," she said.

Fernande had a drink, too. Then I had another drink. This wasn't the first time I had done it. I had been drinking rum for the last few days, but only in tea, so that Edith took it for granted when my breath smelled of rum. I arranged it cleverly; there was only a spoonful of tea to a cup of rum. On the French Riviera once, in Nice, a bartender in the cathedral-like bar at the Hotel Negresco told me that the French drink cognac to down a rebellious conscience, and the English drink straight gin, but that nothing quiets a bad conscience so well as rum. I'd like to let him know, now—he was right. Only I have one thing to add to his prescription—you need a lot of rum. An awful lot. Or, rather, that depends on how bad the conscience is. Up to the time Hilda asked Fernande questions, one or two glasses were enough. After that I needed much, much more. There were one or two nights when I needed such an enormous amount that I'm afraid to write down how much. Edith drank, too. One night we both drank so much that we lay together in bed and cried loudly. Then we started to laugh so about having cried, that our neighbor began frantically hammering on the wall with his fists. We cried because that night was the first time we played the game, "If we had another chance to be born." I'd read in a book of sayings from the works of famous men that, speaking about life in one of his books, Thomas Carlyle had said, "No second chance for us forever more!" The game grew out of that. What would it be like if we had a second chance, after all? If we came into the world again?

We had worked out to the smallest detail the scene in which, young and happy, we'd go hand in hand to the church and be married by the priest. I'd be twenty-six, and she nineteen. My dear mother always said that the ideal difference in age between husband and wife was seven years. We drank, and imagined the way she would be dressed. We conjured up the beautiful white silk bridal gown, the long train, the veil, the myrtle leaves in her red hair, the big white bouquet in her white-gloved hands, her white stockings, her white shoes. We had another drink and described my full-dress suit, my white-kid gloves, my top hat, my smoothly shaved chin, my youth. We decided that I should even have a pedicure the day before the wedding. I would have a little brown mustache, and a white carnation in my buttonhole—and all this would take place in our native land, in Hungary, not in noisy Budapest, but in a quiet little town in the mountains near which we would have a little farm. And we only needed another half glass of rum apiece to hear the organ play the wedding march. That was when we both began crying. Then we were silent with bated breath, while our spirits listened to the church organ playing the wedding march. You could hear it very clearly. We broke into the loud laughter when it came out that she had heard Lohengrin's wedding march with the ears of her mind, but I had been listening to Mendelssohn. Then Edith said something I can't forget.

She said, "No, that's not good enough. If we could be born again, we wouldn't be lovers. We would be brother and sister. Then we would *only* love each other, and no such harm could come to us as has come to us in this life."

We got up regularly now about the time Fernande came home from work, half-past six in the evening. She waited while we dressed, telling us meanwhile about the customers—who had been in the shop and who had ordered what lingerie. My wife hadn't asked her any questions since that first time. She treated Fernande just as before. There was no difference at all. Fernande observed my wife very carefully. She said Hilda was just as calm as ever, but she could see clearly that she knew all about it. Edith wouldn't believe it.

"How can you tell that she knows all about it?"

"I can see she does."

"But how? From what?"

She shrugged her shoulders.

"I can see it. I'd be willing to swear she knows it all, if you like."

"Dr. Knopfler," I said.

"That's possible," Edith said.

The three of us went to dinner together in the delicatessen around the corner, as we did every evening. And came home early. To drink rum. They both drank with me because I "was allowed to," and—because I drank most. I had no fear of death any more. I've often thought what a great, world-famous psychiatrist I could become if I were able to tell what had made it disappear. In so short a time. Because it was completely gone. Not only my fear of death but my overevaluation of life. Edith and I read together in the Book of Job, "Remember that my life is wind." We understood that and loved it. How many men's spirits I could make easier if I knew what had made my desire to go on living at any price—at any price at all—disappear. But I don't know what made it disappear. Of itself? From the rum? From happiness? From my terribly fast pulse— over a hundred now—from the uneven, skipping heartbeats? Or from the approach of death?

The attack, the second attack, was far worse than the first, that time at the Hotel Grindale. And the character of it was different from the first, because this one was accompanied by what seemed to be unbearable pain. I would like to record on exactly which day of my free life this attack began, but I can't remember how many days of happiness I had spent. Six . . . or ten? I don't know—days and nights all flowed together so. Sometimes we slept in the daytime, and sat in a bar at night, or went walking. Sometimes we didn't get out of bed for forty-eight hours at a stretch. Is it possible that it was three days and ten nights?

The attack came toward daybreak this time, too. Out of my torture I heard telephoning, and saw Edith's and Fernande's faces bent over me, and later between them the martyr face of Dr. Knopfler with its scanty beard.

And there were needles sterilized again, and again I was stuck in the thigh and arm . . . and Fernande sobbed hysterically and the others calmed her irritably . . . and I began to feel a little drowsy from the morphine. They didn't want me to hear, but I did hear the doctor telling Edith that it was natural for this to happen with the kind of life I'd been living, and it was only a wonder it hadn't happened sooner. Edith said something about its all being her fault, that she was to blame, but Dr. Knopfler reassured her, saying, no, it was not her fault, it was entirely mine, because he had told me precisely what was permitted and what was not. Outwardly everything was like the first time, except that this time there was no oxygen tent. Instead of that, two strange men came, carrying long poles wrapped in canvas, which turned out to be a stretcher. They lifted me out of bed and laid me on the stretcher. I knew that this meant the hospital, but I didn't protest. They covered me up and put a pillow under my head. Before they took me out into the hall, Fernande, her eyes red with weeping, wiped my forehead and face tenderly with a handkerchief soaked in eau de cologne. I remember that in my misery I whispered to her that the pillow under my head didn't belong to us, but to Mrs. Glicksman, from whom we had rented the room, and that it would have to be returned to her. Fernande promised and began to cry all over again. Dr. Knopfler turned on her brutally and scolded her in French. I couldn't understand what he said, because he spoke French badly and with a heavy accent.

In the hospital they laid me on a very high bed in a small room. Three thick pipes, painted to match the walls, ran across the room along the ceiling over the bed. I saw a young doctor and a nurse, too. Edith sat beside the bed and held my hand. Fernande went away, because it was morning now and she had to go to work. Before she went, though, she reassured me by saying she would come back to see me after six that evening and would take the pillow back to Mrs. Glicksman then. The two of them, Edith and Fernande, whispered together at the door. Without hearing a word, I knew what they were talking about. Dr. Knopfler went over to them while they were talking, and I distinctly caught the words, "I absolutely forbid it."

It was then that it became clear to me that they were discussing whether or not Fernande should tell my wife what had happened. I was grateful to Dr. Knopfler for forbidding it. Although it was natural he should. I understood enough about my illness by now to know that any excitement must be avoided.

Fernande went, and Edith and Dr. Knopfler left the room, too. I was alone with the hospital nurse, who was sitting in an armchair next to the window and looking out. I could hear muffled talking out in the hall, even though the speakers were trying to whisper so I wouldn't hear. I even gathered from their speech that they were still discussing whether my wife should be told; but this time the hospital intern was arguing with Dr. Knopfler and there was a third, unfamiliar male voice—I don't know whose. Edith wasn't taking part in the discussion. I could hear that Dr. Knopfler was getting excited. He was speaking louder than he should have. He said they shouldn't let my wife know because they—the hospital doctors—didn't know the circumstances under which my illness had started, and if my wife came here now it might mean a degree of excitement fatal to me.

"But those are the rules," the third voice said.

Dr. Knopfler said something to the effect that he wanted them to understand that this man was married and had gotten the attack early in the morning in bed with his mistress, that his wife had no idea that he had a mistress with whom he was sleeping, and if it all came out now, and his wife appeared here, even if she only came into my room and didn't make a scene, or even if I only realized that she'd been told the whole thing, he, Dr. Knopfler, would not vouch for what would happen and would consider it a great mistake from a medical viewpoint.

"Orders," the voice said, and the other doctor said something, too, and I heard words like, "Routine . . . duty . . . law . . ."

Dr. Knopfler only repeated stubbornly, "I won't permit it. I won't permit it."

In my great misery, I was unjust enough to think that perhaps he wasn't trying to protect me at all, but to save Edith from a scandal. The hospital interns began to say something about Dr. Knopfler's having no right to walk into the hospital and give orders, and it would be best for him to go away. It must have been a nasty argument, because in the heat of the fight I caught both the doctors calling Dr. Knopfler "alien" and "refugee." Dr. Knopfler was getting too noisy, and one of the interns grew noisy, too, and snapped out at him, "Stop yelling!"

"I'll yell if I like," Dr. Knopfler shouted.

"I'll have you thrown out," the intern said in a furious whisper. Thanks to the morphine, I was growing sleepier minute by minute, and so I didn't hear how the argument ended.

CHAPTER SEVENTEEN

I WRITE; from one to two hours every day, I cover these sheets of paper. I have to stay in bed all the time. At first the doctors didn't want to let me write down the story of a period so upsetting to me. But Edith begged them at my request, until they conferred about it, and gave me permission. I remembered an old story then that my dear mother used to tell about a friend of hers who was dying. This man was strictly forbidden alcohol in any form. Once he suddenly asked his family for a glass of beer. They refused, in shocked surprise. But, after a consultation, the doctors said, "All right, let him have the beer."

"How much?" asked the family.

"As much as he wants," said the doctors.

It seems that it's all one with me now, too. So, then, I am writing this in bed. Fernande brought a little bed table from Macy's. She went to buy it because Edith wouldn't stir from here. I don't know what to call all these pages I've covered with writing, and the ones I still hope to cover. I only know that an inner compulsion forces me to write them. For one last time before he passes away, the reporter in me has risen up to put on paper all that has happened. You can't be a reporter for thirty years without its leaving its mark. Should I call it "A Fragment from an Autobiography?" Or diary? Self-portrait? In case I should live a few months longer (of which there's very little chance) I'll have a try at finding a publisher, and see if I can have it published in book form. If not, then I'll entrust it to Edith. Herewith I present this manuscript to her. It is my first and last literary work. Though I'm afraid it's still only a job of reporting. But . . . what is literature? I believe it's only a very honest reporting job. Dickens, Flaubert, Zola, Sinclair Lewis, Hemingway? Superb reporters. The title will be *Self-Portrait of a Coward* or *The Man Who Didn't Want to Die*. Or some other title. They say it's more important what kind of title a book has in America than back in Europe.

When I'd written down the confession Hilda made about her first husband that time on Long Island, I gave Edith those pages to read.

"Oh, I know," she said.

"What?"

"The story about them."

"Since when?"

"Oh, a long time."

"Where did you hear it?"

"They were telling it in Hollywood."

"And up to this day you've never mentioned to me that you knew it?"

"Why should I have?"

There are no secrets, and the world is small. Smaller than we think.

"But it wasn't the way you've written it," she said.

"I wrote it the way Hilda told it to me."

"I'm sure that's the way she told it. But that isn't the way it was."

"How was it, then?"

"Her husband really had one foot in jail."

"That's just what I wrote."

"And it's true, too. He committed suicide. Threw himself out of a hotel window."

"That's exactly what I wrote. What's wrong with it?"

"The way it goes on. The woman's story."

"In what way?"

She glanced at me reluctantly. I encouraged her.

"Go on. Go on . . . it's all the same now, anyhow."

"All right, I'll tell you, but only because it may relieve your mind."

She was still reluctant.

"Well?" I urged her.

"The woman lied to you."

"About what?"

"Darling," she said, "that woman spent two years in jail."

"For what?"

"I don't know exactly. For the same reason that made her husband jump from the twentieth floor. But she was locked up."

I stared in front of me. I think I was smiling. Frankly, I felt sorry for Hilda—because I simply can't express how kind and affectionate she had been to me.

"How do you know all this?" I asked.

"It's the truth. Don't ask me about it, just take my word for it. There are files on the whole thing; I even know at what lawyer's. But it's not worth stirring up the whole story. If I tell you it's true, it's true. It wasn't such a crime to leave a woman like that. I don't say that because she was in jail, but because she concealed it from you. Do you really think a woman like that— good-looking, not too old, with her own house, and a prosperous little business—would have grabbed so greedily at marriage with a man she hardly knew if there weren't some little blemish on her past?"

I didn't tell her that the same idea had occurred to me, too. Nevertheless, for a moment, I had the feeling that what I had just heard was not true, and that Edith had only said it to ease my conscience. I made no effort to find out—I had no wish to know—whether or not the story was true. At heart, I was always grateful to Hilda.

"A decent woman, a thoroughly good woman," I said.

"Possibly. Certainly, if you say so."

She added with a bitter little smile, "I'm not decent. Or thoroughly good, either."

"You're more," I said. "You're you."

"Yes, that's the hell of it," she answered.

That same afternoon the young intern interrupted my writing. He came into my room.

"We've decided to let your wife visit you for a little while," he said. "Just a few minutes."

"Now?"

"Now."

He waited for results, for an answer. I was calm.

"Of course," I said. "Where is Edith?"

"She's up in the nurse's dormitory, sleeping. She hasn't slept at all for the last few nights. Your wife is waiting outside. I'll bring her in, if it's all right with you. And if you don't mind, I'll stay around—somewhere in the background."

I laid down my fountain pen and nodded agreement.

Hilda came in. You could clearly see the effects of what had happened to her. That is, what I had done to her. Even so, an automatic smile was fixed on her face. The same smile she used for selling silk panties to rich ladies.

"Sit down, Hilda."

She tried to sit on the edge of the bed, but she couldn't, because the bed was too high. We both smiled at that. The doctor pushed an armchair over for her.

She spoke quietly. "The doctor says your condition is satisfactory."

She glanced at the doctor for approval. The intern answered diplomatically.

"That was the condition this morning. We'll examine him again this evening."

Hilda looked around the little room.

"Do you have everything you need?"

"Oh, yes."

"Wouldn't you prefer a bigger room?"

"No, no."

"Shall I send you anything? Or bring anything? Can't I do something?"

"He has everything he needs," the doctor said.

"Something to eat or drink, something to wear?"

"Everything," the doctor said.

We were silent. I stared straight ahead of me into the air. Hilda watched me fixedly, didn't take her eyes off me for a long time—without any reproach or criticism in her expression, I must admit—kindly, sympathetic, fond. That continued for a while. Then the doctor glanced at his wrist watch. That was meant for Hilda, I knew. Hilda turned to the doctor.

"When can I come again?"

"Telephone the morning of the day you want to come. We'll tell you."

"Thank you."

The doctor went to the door, to urge Hilda on her way. Hilda bent over me.

"Darling," she said softly.

She kissed my forehead tenderly and went. When she was still in the doorway, I saw her take out her handkerchief. I sighed deeply, and went on writing, with the idea that my time was limited and I still had a lot to put down—this first visit of my wife's, too, to point out how decently she had acted. I hadn't deserved it of her.

About two days later, around four in the afternoon, I was writing industriously, and Edith was sitting beside my bed, when the nurse came in.

"Your wife is here," she said.

"With the doctor's permission?" Edith asked.

"Yes. He brought her this far and said I should stay in the room with her. She's only allowed to stay five minutes."

I looked helplessly at Edith. I wasn't prepared for the two of them meeting ever again in their lives.

"All right," Edith said, and went out with the nurse. I pushed the written pages aside, leaned my head back on my pillow, and waited. I waited for a long time, but no one came. Suddenly, I heard a scream out in the corridor. Nowhere near my room. The nurse was screaming. She called out a name.

"Bill! Bill!"

A man's voice answered.

"Coming!"

Strange sounds, like dull thuds, reached the room from the corridor. As though a sack of flour or an over-stuffed armchair was being thrown around. I didn't know what it was at first. Then I realized that it sounded like silent wrestling. The nurse called shrilly to the same Bill.

"Bill . . . hurry!"

"Coming," Bill said. He came, and through the nurse's hysterical crying, you could hear him breath-lessly reasoning with the wrestlers. "My dear women! Now . . . what's going on here, anyhow? Now, really, ladies!"

Then you could hear one single scream. That was Edith screaming. Then silence. Then men's and wo-

men's voices again. One voice kept on saying uninterruptedly, "Ladies . . . gentlemen . . . for God's
sake! You're in a hospital!"

A new voice rang out, vigorous and authoritative.

"Get out of here, all of you. Miss Brown, take this
girl to my office. That cut has to be washed out. Stitches
taken and a bandage put on."

It grew quiet. Later I learned what had happened.
When Edith left my room, she walked along the short
wing of the hall, at the end of which my room was. At
the other end, where the wing joined the main corridor, Hilda was standing, waiting. Edith was forced to
walk past Hilda, and as she did, Hilda lunged at her.
Hilda is a big, muscular woman. She didn't say a word,
and Edith didn't let out a sound, either. They wrestled
silently. Hilda threw Edith down on the floor, and
when the hospital attendant named Bill came to
Edith's aid, Hilda was holding her by the throat and
choking her. This Bill and the nurse held Hilda down.
But by that time Edith's face was bleeding. As soon as
Hilda realized that they were going to wrench her victim out of her grasp, she bit Edith in the face. When
I saw Edith again later, her face was concealed in band-
ages, as well covered as a surgeon in the operating
room, or a nurse caring for a pampered infant.

I found that very depressing, although it didn't surprise me. Nothing surprises me any more, nothing up-
sets me. Dr. Knopfler doesn't have to protect me from
exciting scenes or dramatic events. Strange, but I have
only a single worry left. To get down on paper all that

has happened to me in these less than ninety days. To end the last chapter of my autobiography before they give me *that* injection of morphine from which I will not awaken. I always loved my profession, journalism. But I would never have believed that the desire to be a reporter again would ever grow to such proportions, and be such complete consolation. Would I ever have believed that the last desire of my life would be to do a full and honest reporting job?

In spite of what happened, I gather that my wife comes to the hospital every day, but that they won't let her come to see me. Edith doesn't budge from my side. Sometimes when I watch her silently I think she is a saint. At such moments, lost in thought, I can understand how, once upon a time, people confused saints with witches, and the church afterward canonized the very people it had once burned at the stake.

The days pass. They move as swiftly "as a weaver's shuttle." And I know that the only way I will leave this place is when I am carried out feet first. All for nothing, I was alternately clever and stupid, cautious and daring, cruel and softhearted, decent and mean—none of it helped. The unknown red-haired girl who, at a Swiss station, accidentally got into the compartment in which I was traveling murdered me in spite of it—by no other means than making me love her and loving me in return—by nothing else. She couldn't help it, and I no longer regret what happened. I was happy with her, and there are still whole minutes when I close my eyes and forget all that's wrong, and am happy just because she's sitting beside me.

I don't know how many more days I will have to write this report, but—for as long as I go on writing—every day when I begin to write, I call back to mind that instant on the Swiss-Italian frontier when the Fascist officer barked his question at me.

"Religion?"

And the moment when the officer went out. And the Finnish consul addressed me. And a strange, red-haired girl, sitting in the corner, looked at me. Perhaps she had looked at me before, but the first time I noticed that she was gazing in my eyes was when the consul spoke to me. Perhaps I only imagine it, but every time I conjure up that moment, I believe that even then I knew everything that would happen.

CHAPTER EIGHTEEN

> The preceding seventeen chapters of the
> manuscript published here reached the
> man named as author of this book with
> an accompanying letter. This letter should
> properly be the preface to the book. But
> the author thought it better to make it the
> last chapter.

Dear Sir:

I am a compatriot of yours. You don't know me. My
name is Edith Knopfler. My husband is Dr. Andrew
Knopfler, a doctor practicing in New York. He is Austrian by birth. I decided to send you this manuscript
after discussing the matter with him, and with his permission. I am sure you will not lay these sheets aside
without reading them. We know that you have lived
here in New York for years, and that you are in intimate contact with our small Hungarian refugee col-
ony. You have often shown that you feel yourself to be
one of us—that's why I am taking the liberty of speaking to you as a friend.

I was given the manuscript in the E. N. W. hospital
by the man who wrote it. My husband is a person of
saintlike qualities. He is a theosophist, a spiritualist.
He didn't like the man who wrote this manuscript. I

loved him. In my husband's opinion, he was a weak and cruel man. Perhaps he was. But I cannot blame him for it, because he was only weak about me, and he was crueler to himself than to me or to his wife. My husband never felt any sympathy for him, never, even for an instant. But I can't criticize him, because I loved him from the first moment I saw him, and will always love him, not for this reason or that, but because I can't not love him, and because I've been more than ever in love with him since he died—because of me. For all his egotism, he did die because he loved me. That's a fact which can't be denied.

Please make whatever use of this manuscript you see fit. If you decide to publish it, polish it up. I don't understand these things, but my husband says that the style must be smoothed down, the names changed— that is very important—the story divided into chapters, and so on. For my part I have only one request. I beg of you not to soften or embellish my character in the story, because the man who wrote these things about me was almost always right in his criticism. If I had wanted to appear to better advantage in the story, I would have left out certain things in the manuscript.

I wouldn't like you to add anything to the script, except to say just at the end that after his death I married Dr. Andrew Knopfler. He is a person of very liberal ideas. He knows I never loved anyone as I loved this man, yet he married me in spite of it, and gives me complete liberty to build what you might call a shrine to the man's memory. Even though, as I said, he didn't ever like him, and would be happiest if I could forget him.

Once in the hospital, the man told me half jokingly to send you the manuscript if he died. He had read your books ever since he was a young man and somehow he felt that the best place for the confessions of a man like himself would be in a writer's hands. A short time ago I bought Somerset Maugham's new book, *The Razor's Edge*. There I found the following lines: "People do tell a writer things that they don't tell others . . . and, seeing themselves as it were characters in a novel, are ready to be as open with him as they imagine are to him the characters of his invention." It was only after I read these lines that I fully understood the half-joking, half-serious suggestion of the writer of these notes.

As you'll see in the manuscript, he suggested various titles for these biographical confessions. But I, with my unliterary mind, don't like any of them, because he abuses and belittles himself in them all.

He died on March 31, 1940. He didn't live to see the real war, the occupation of Norway, Denmark, Holland, and Belgium, the fall of France, or Dunkirk, or the German invasion of Russia, or Pearl Harbor, or America's entry into the war. For some time, I can't deny, my husband and I have been doubtful as to whether we ought to send you this manuscript, after all—just because of these world-shaking events. My husband says that today, when death is carrying on its triumphant orgy throughout the world, the sound of a little private struggle with death, like this one, is too soft to be heard. But lately we've been talking so much again about whether I ought to carry out his wishes or not that I've begun to lie awake nights. I've hardly slept for weeks now, and I feel that my nerves are giving way, and that I won't have any peace until I do what this man once asked of me. The wish of a dead person has an awful strength.

Please drop me a line as soon as you receive the manuscript. I think I'll sleep comparatively peacefully that night, for the first time in a long while.

Sincerely yours,

Edith Knopfler

ABOUT THE AUTHOR

FERENC MOLNAR *was born in Budapest, Hungary. His novels, short stories, and plays have delighted readers in many countries. Seventeen of the plays have been produced on Broadway, among them* Liliom, The Guardsman, The Play's the Thing, The Swan, The Devil, *and* The Good Fairy.

Mr. Molnar is now living in the United States, awaiting his final citizenship papers. Farewell My Heart *is the first book he has written with an American setting.*